DUDLEY PUBLIC

POP!

MITCH JOHNSON

Orion

ORION CHILDREN'S BOOKS

First published in Great Britain in 2020 by Hodder & Stoughton

1 3 5 7 9 10 8 6 4 2

A CIP catalogue record for this book
is available from the British Library.

ISBN 978 1 510 10761 8

Typeset in ITC Berkeley by Hewer Text UK Ltd, Edinburgh

Printed and bound by CPI Group (UK) Ltd, Croydon CR0 4YY

The paper and board used in this book
are made from wood from responsible sources.

Orion Children's Books
An imprint of
Hachette Children's Group
Part of Hodder & Stoughton
Carmelite House
50 Victoria Embankment
London, EC4Y 0DZ

An Hachette UK Company
www.hachette.co.uk

www.hachettechildrens.co.uk

The good Earth – we could have saved it, but we were too damn cheap and lazy.*

Kurt Vonnegut, *A Man Without a Country*

Disclaimer

Mac-Tonic™, Macfarlane's Miracle Tonic™ and M-T™ are all trademarks of The Mac-Tonic™ Corporation. What follows is an unauthorized account of what has come to be known as the Great Thirst. The Mac-Tonic™ Corporation refutes the allegations made herein, and is committed to prosecuting its author and disseminators to the fullest extent of the law.

The Mac-Tonic™ Corporation strongly advises against reading this seditious material.

Alexander Greenberg, Chief Attorney
of The Mac-Tonic™ Corporation

PROLOGUE

Rendezvous at 40,000 Feet

Lyle Funderburk sipped a glass of ice-cold Mac-Tonic™, on the way back from a conference in Japan. He swirled the chipped ice around his tumbler, deep in thought. The conference had gone well. Japan was a good territory – one of the best – but it could be better, more profitable, and he knew it. *But how?* He took another sip of the sickly-sweet soda and let the bubbles pop on his tongue. He peered down at the Pacific Ocean 40,000 feet below, stretched out like a giant, glistening waste of space, but inspiration didn't strike.

An air hostess appeared and replaced his glass of Mac-Tonic™ before the ice had chance to melt and dilute the soda. The new beverage was served at exactly 34 degrees Fahrenheit. The ice had been perfectly chipped by hand; it was one of the many qualities required of a hostess, right up there with possessing an understanding of guests' needs that bordered on the telepathic. And being young, of course. When it came to the Mac-Tonic™

fleet, anyone over twenty-five had about as much chance of taking off as a refrigerator bolted to the floor.

The air hostess smiled sweetly, or sweetened her permanently sweet smile, and glided away.

Lyle Funderburk allowed himself to be distracted by her only for a moment. Time is money, after all. He checked his watch. The jet was making excellent time for his lunch appointment with Senator McVeigh.

But unbeknownst to Lyle Funderburk, the jet was speeding towards something that threatened to destroy them all. Because, travelling from California to Shanghai, straight across the Pacific in the opposite direction, was another private jet. Its sole passenger was Lewie Hewitt. He sat in the luxury of a deep leather seat, swirling a glass of Mac-Tonic™ that had been cooled to the exact temperature of 34 degrees Fahrenheit by a young, smiling air hostess. He was thinking about money, and how he could make more of it.

Lyle and Lewie knew each other well. They were colleagues and enemies; either of them might feasibly become CEO of The Mac-Tonic™ Corporation if Dwight Eagleman ever retired or moved to another company or *just dropped dead already*. Lyle was Head of International Marketing and Branding; Lewie was Head of Global

Operations. They didn't expect to be meeting each other so soon. Their next scheduled face-to-face wasn't until the following month, at the annual Mac-Tonic™ shareholders' convention in New York City.

But as things turned out, they had an unscheduled rendezvous at 40,000 feet.

The pilots spotted each other at the last second – were close enough to recognize the terror in the other's eyes – before instinctively snatching at the controls in a futile attempt to avoid a collision. They sheered away, forcing their wings to meet like two swords clashing in battle. The wings were ripped off. The planes spiralled out of the sky, trailing thick clouds of black smoke behind them in a revolving helix.

In a way, it was beautiful, but there was no one there to admire it. The nearest civilization was a thousand miles away.

Lyle and Lewie couldn't believe what was happening. They were used to being in control, to wielding unimaginable power, and so to find themselves plummeting towards the Pacific Ocean, each with only a screaming air hostess for company, was difficult to comprehend.

I can't die now, they both thought, separately. *If I die now, I'll never become CEO.*

They wondered who would be promoted into their positions, after their deaths. *Martin DeWitt? Donnie Holland? Alexander Greenberg?* None of them deserved such seniority in the company. None of them deserved to know what they knew.

Then they thought about their wives. More specifically, about whom their wives would remarry. They both suspected it would be Randy van de Velde, the wily old Texan.

Then they thought about their kids, and wondered why they had ever included them in their wills. No doubt they would squander the fortunes their fathers had worked so tirelessly and ruthlessly to accumulate.

Their only consolation, as the jets hurtled towards the water below, was that the company would prevail. Its worker bees might perish, but the colony would survive. The sweet stuff would continue to flow. The Mac-Tonic™ Corporation would prosper.

They hit the water smiling.

What they didn't know, of course, was who was in the other jet. No single person could be entrusted with something as valuable as the Mac-Tonic™ formula, and so two executives were entrusted with half each. Lyle Funderburk and Lewie Hewitt were the two keepers of the secret. As a precaution, they were not allowed to travel together, in case their car rolled down the side of a mountain, or their yacht sank, or their helicopter fell from the sky.

But no one had considered the possibility that two jets might collide in mid-air.

The odds must have been a trillion to one.

Some guys are just unlucky, I guess.

And so, as the last of the wreckage slipped beneath the waves, in the middle of the greatest expanse of water on Earth, the Great Thirst began.

North Nitch, California

Chuckie de la Cruz stole one hundred dollars from the bank and slipped it into his pocket, and Queenie watched him do it.

Her brother always cheated, as brothers always do, but Queenie didn't say a word. The more money he had, the more money she could take from him: he was financing his own downfall. All Queenie needed was for Chuckie to think he was getting away with it, and so she pretended to pay attention to the sounds of the TV drifting through the open window – something dull about environmental protests farther up the coast. When Chuckie glanced up, Queenie made sure her eyes were fixed on the brown, litter-strewn ocean beyond the back porch railings.

'Your go,' Queenie said.

Chuckie picked up the dice and rolled them across the board. Queenie quickly calculated where he was going to land and tried to hide her smile. Chuckie counted the spaces out one by one with his top hat token (which he insisted on calling a cowboy hat) and only slowed down on the penultimate property. He glanced at Queenie, but she was watching all right.

'Pay up,' Queenie said.

Chuckie scowled. 'How much?'

'Two hundred.'

'What?!'

'I own all the railroads, so that'll be two hundred dollars. Please.'

'How do you own so much stuff already?' Chuckie said, reaching for the bank. 'I swear you must be cheating . . .'

Queenie lost her cool.

'Use *your* money, dummy, not the bank's! I know you have difficulty telling them apart sometimes.'

Chuckie froze. 'What are you trying to say?'

Queenie rolled her eyes. 'Don't play stupid.'

'I'm not!'

'All right, then stop *being* stupid. I know you're cheating! It's obvious; there are bills spilling out of your pockets!'

Chuckie looked down at the banknotes tumbling from his shorts. His face went from shock to confusion to anger like a traffic light. And then he launched himself at Queenie.

Playing Monopoly was one of only two things Queenie and Chuckie ever did together: the other was fighting, and they probably only played Monopoly because it was almost guaranteed to end in a fight. As a result, Queenie was ready for Chuckie's attack; she rolled out of the way and jumped down the porch steps on to the sand below. But anger made Chuckie surprisingly fast, and he barrelled after Queenie in a flurry of money, knocking her backwards and landing on her chest. His podgy hands were still clutching hundred-dollar bills, and he tried to force them into Queenie's mouth.

'You want my money? Here, eat it!'

Queenie twisted her head this way and that, struggling to dislodge her brother. But Chuckie was a big boy; it was like being sat on by a juvenile elephant. She was going to have to fight dirty.

She reached out to the side, grabbed a handful of sand and threw it in Chuckie's face. He rolled away, spitting and spluttering and rubbing his eyes.

'Ma!' he yelled, staggering towards the house. 'Ma!'

He crawled up the broken steps, across the bleached boards of the porch and blundered through the back door.

For a moment, Queenie just lay there panting, looking at the house through a tangle of dark hair. It looked like a shipwreck that had washed up to be battered by the elements. The boards twisted away from the walls, the back porch sagged and the shutters were a strong fart from coming away completely. The sky was often hazy with the fumes from a nearby industrial waste incinerator, and every surface held a smear of soot. A sewage pipe emerged from the sand beside the house and ran on rusty fixings to the water's edge, where it dribbled its contents into the ocean. The waves were lazy and brown and fizzed creamy foam up the sand, carrying trash that spiteful currents conspired to channel into the bay. The whole thing looked like an arcade coin-pusher, constantly advancing and retreating, carrying prizes that nobody wanted to win.

This is not what I imagined when Ma said we'd be moving to California, Queenie thought, for the hundredth time. *No wonder I'd never heard of North Nitch.*

North Nitch wasn't in any of the guidebooks or travel brochures. Most maps left it off altogether. There were no blue skies or white beaches, no statuesque muscle men newly cast in bronze, no goddesses in hot pants gliding by on rollerblades. There were no beach parties or barbecues (although someone did set fire to a shopping cart once). No glistening lifeguards, or fancy seafood restaurants, or street performers. There was no one in aviators or bug-eye sunglasses, endlessly reflecting the beauty of the people and the place. Groups of teenagers didn't lounge around, having the time of their lives, sipping on ice-cold bottles of Mac-Tonic™ that beaded in the sun but never dripped to leave ugly blemishes on the sand.

Life was nothing like a commercial in North Nitch, California, but it was the place Queenie de la Cruz was supposed to call home.

She wandered away from the house, towards the water, and sat on an upturned plastic crate. It was fifty-fifty whether Ma would come for her or not, but there was no way she'd come as far as the water's edge, not even to shut Chuckie up. Queenie put her chin in her hands and watched as the sun went down.

Some evenings, the sun just slid below the horizon without a whimper, like a coin fed into a slot. But other times, like this evening, it spilled itself across the water in a red flood, throwing pink light over everything on the shore: the coffee cups and chunks of polystyrene; the garden chairs tangled in fishing wire; the plastic bottles that looked like dead fish.

Sometimes, Queenie missed the sunsets in Kansas. It was still a clear run to the sun here, but the space in between was a different kind of empty. It used to feel like she could walk all the way to the horizon, through the bristling cornfields and yawning nothingness, if only she had the time. But here, it was like standing at the edge of something impassable. It felt like she'd already come as far as she was ever going to go, even though there was so much out there that she still wanted to explore.

And it was made worse by the nostalgia of Kansas. At least her pa had been around back then, and they'd been a complete family, no matter how dysfunctional. But then he'd gotten drunk (again), and mistook the thud of hailstones on the trailer roof for golf balls from the neighbouring driving range (again), and climbed on to the roof with a putter, yelling 'Return to sender!' (again), and taken a swing at one of the oversized hailstones just as a bolt of lightning forked through the sky.

The house in North Nitch had seemed like a good place to go after that – even if the estranged uncle who'd left it to the de la Cruz family in his will was supposed to hate them.

It wasn't until they arrived that they realized he'd left them the place *because* he hated them. It was barely habitable.

Watching the bloody sunset, Queenie sighed at the memory and nudged an empty Mac-Tonic™ bottle with her foot. She had an urge to go somewhere, to do something, but the thought of trudging across the litter-strewn landscape made the effort seem pointless. She was so bored she almost wished Ma would come out and holler at her for fighting Chuckie, but the house behind her remained dark and silent except for the flicker and murmur of the TV.

The sight of so many Mac-Tonic™ bottles was making Queenie thirsty, and she was just about to get up and head home when she saw a couple of people making their way along the shoreline. This in itself was pretty bizarre – nobody ever visited this stretch of beach – but what they were doing was even stranger. The two people shuffled along at an impossibly slow pace, stopping every second or so to collect a piece of trash and drop it into one of the sacks they were carrying.

Queenie was transfixed. She'd never seen anything quite like it before in her life.

As the two people got closer, Queenie could see that one was a man, and one was a woman. The man had a long grey ponytail that reached down to the small of his back, and glasses with small circular lenses that flashed red in the light of the setting sun. The woman wore a purple bandana tied around her head, and a tie-dye T-shirt that hung beyond her knees. As the couple approached Queenie, they smiled and waved at the same time. Without realizing it, Queenie had gotten off the crate and taken a step towards them.

'What are you doing?' she asked.

The couple stopped, but they kept smiling.

'We're picking up trash,' the woman said. She held out a fresh bag. 'Wanna join in?'

Queenie shook her head, squinting into the sun. 'No, I mean, I can see what you're doing, but why?'

The man picked up a Mac-Tonic™ bottle and turned it over in his hands.

'We're tidying up.'

Queenie was still struggling with the concept.

'But it isn't your trash.'

He smiled and dropped the bottle into his bag. 'But it is our problem.'

'But it'll just wash up again,' Queenie said. 'No matter how much you pick up, there will always be more.'

The man shrugged. 'All the more reason to make a start, I guess.'

'Are you sure you don't wanna join in?' the woman asked. 'It's your world too.'

Queenie wasn't quite sure what to say to that. She'd never thought of anywhere beyond her bedroom as her world, and she didn't own anything that someone hadn't given away or left behind: even her sneakers were from a thrift store. The world didn't belong to anybody, except for maybe a big company like Mac-Tonic™, but certainly not people like her. *Did it?*

The question was too difficult to answer, so she asked one instead.

'Are you two with those people from the news? The ones protesting?'

The woman smiled warmly. 'That's right. I'm Linda, and this is Max, and we're—'

'Hippies!' Chuckie shouted.

Queenie spun round. Chuckie was standing on the porch, pointing a finger in her direction.

'Ma! Come quick! We've got hippies!'

Ma had warned them about tree-hugging, drug-smoking, daydreaming hippies before they set off for

14

California. Apparently, California had a real problem with them. An infestation, she'd called it. Although she'd never mentioned anything about litter picking.

Max and Linda looked a bit bemused, but their eyes filled with fear when Ma's massive frame appeared on the back porch brandishing a broom.

'Queenie!' she hollered. 'Get away from those hippies! Don't take nothing from them!'

Queenie shook her head and covered her face with a hand. When she took it away a few moments later, Max and Linda were scrambling over a nearby sand dune, dragging their bags of trash behind them. Ma kept the broom raised until they'd disappeared over the other side. Then she leaned it by the back door and went inside.

'Way to go, Ma!' Chuckie said, hurrying after her. 'You showed them!'

Queenie looked around at the tide of Mac-Tonic™ bottles Max and Linda had been about to collect. One of them had dropped a thin roll of garbage bags during their escape, and Queenie bent down to pick it up. For a crazy moment, she thought about carrying on where they'd left off. But then Chuckie's voice sliced the thought in half.

'Queenie! Ma says get your scrawny hide in here right now!'

Queenie turned towards the house. The moon was rising directly above it. It looked like a giant red bottle cap, with a circle of teeth around the circumference and the Mac-Tonic™ logo looping across the middle. Apparently, many years before, the moon had just been a blank, stupid face. But Queenie didn't know about that.

The sight of it made her think about the trash behind her, and the roll of bags clutched in her fist.

But more than anything, it made her thirsty.

Queenie stopped on the porch and glanced back at the shore, at the blanket of plastic trash.

What a dump, she thought.

Then she went into the dilapidated house and fetched a Mac-Tonic™ from the refrigerator.

Welcome to Mac-Tonic™

Dwight Eagleman was scalping strawberries with an ivory-handled knife when his secretary entered the office. She moved with purpose without seeming hurried, and spoke with an economy of words that Dwight Eagleman valued. Once upon a time, before she turned twenty-five, she had been an air hostess on a Mac-Tonic™ jet.

'I've cancelled the Bilderberg meeting,' she said, 'the rest of the board are on their way, and someone from the Madison vault should be here shortly. Senator McVeigh is also on the line. Mr Funderburk stood him up at lunch and he's pretty upset.'

Dwight Eagleman set the knife down between the bowl of strawberries and the bowl of tufty green crowns. He smiled generously, like a busy father making time for a child.

'Thank you, Sarah. Please put him through.'

(The secretary's name was actually Sophie, but Dwight Eagleman was powerful enough to operate his own reality and force people to subscribe to it. Sarah left the room and patched the call through.)

'Alistair,' Dwight Eagleman said, sitting back in his chair and interlocking his fingers in his lap. 'How can I help you?'

Dwight Eagleman's voice was like being warmed by the sun when he wanted it to be, but for Senator McVeigh it felt like getting sunburnt in January. It was strange weather indeed.

'M-Mr Eagleman?' the senator said. He sounded a lot like someone who had spent the last ten minutes demanding to talk to the CEO of a trillion-dollar corporation without expecting or really wanting to talk to the CEO of a trillion-dollar corporation. Like a sheep requesting an audience with whoever has been decimating the flock, only to be introduced to the wolf. 'I . . . er . . . h-had no idea the girl would actually—'

'We can always make time for someone as influential as you, Alistair.'

What he actually meant was that he resented allocating even a nanosecond of his day to Senator McVeigh's petty complaint, but Dwight Eagleman did not need to say such things. Senator McVeigh understood the subtext well enough.

'Well, thank you, Mr Eagleman. It was just that . . . well, I called out of concern, really. I was supposed to meet with Mr Funderburk for lunch and he . . . er . . . failed . . . No, not failed. I mean, he obviously had a more pressing engagement and I just wanted to check that he was . . . er . . . OK.'

It was a pretty lame message, even for a politician.

Dwight Eagleman sat forwards in his chair. He glanced at the clock on the phone display.

'I'm sure there's no need to worry, Alistair. I expect Mr Funderburk had a very good reason for missing your appointment, but I'll be sure to pass on your regards.'

Dwight Eagleman was tempted to give the real reason for Lyle Funderburk's absence, just to hear Senator McVeigh's garbled apology, but he resisted.

'Thank you,' Senator McVeigh said.

It was obvious that he wanted the conversation to be over, but Dwight Eagleman was not the type to leave a lemon unsqueezed when there was still juice to be wrung from it.

'How is your re-election campaign faring?'

This was a dangerous question. Despite however many million people voted for Senator McVeigh, his chances of being re-elected ultimately rested with people like Dwight Eagleman.

'F-fine,' Senator McVeigh said. 'Fairly well.'

'Those protestors aren't making life too difficult, I hope?'

'No. Well, yes. Life would be easier without them, I suppose.'

'OK,' Dwight Eagleman said.

Senator McVeigh knew not to ruin things by saying thank you.

'Did you receive our contribution, by the way?'

'Contribution? I . . . er . . . I'm not sure. Just let me check.'

'Ah,' Dwight Eagleman said, picking up the knife and slicing the top off another strawberry. 'It's the 13th today, isn't it? Our donation is scheduled for the 14th. My mistake.'

'Thank you,' Senator McVeigh said. 'And thank you for your time.'

'Good luck in the election, Alistair. Make sure you

clean up the Californian coast, just like those protestors are demanding.'

'Of course. Thank you. Goodbye.'

The phone rattled in its cradle as the senator rushed to hang up. Dwight Eagleman smiled faintly and shook his head. He trimmed the last strawberry and put it back in the bowl. He never ate strawberries. He just enjoyed scalping them.

Dwight Eagleman rose to his feet and crossed to the floor-to-ceiling window that ran the length of his office. He looked out at the Manhattan skyline. The glass wall curved at either end, giving the room views from Central Park, over the Financial District, to Upper Bay. Dwight Eagleman squinted at the distant figure of the Statue of Liberty and smiled at the giant bottle of Mac-Tonic™ she held aloft.

He thought about Senator McVeigh, and the simple task of silencing a few loudmouth eco-warriors, and wondered whether he would be able to manage it. Perhaps he should fund Smith-Ford's candidacy instead? Or both?

There was a knock at the door. Sarah stepped inside after a moment's pause.

'I've cleared your diary for the rest of the day, Mr

Eagleman.' She lingered on the threshold, uncertain. 'Is everything all right, sir? Has something happened?'

The recipe to the world's most popular soft drink was on the sea floor, somewhere in the Pacific Ocean, along with Lyle Funderburk and Lewie Hewitt, but Dwight Eagleman smiled warmly.

'Everything's fine, Sarah. Thank you.'

Sarah withdrew but, before the door closed, she leaned back into the room.

'Your son is here, by the way.'

Dwight Eagleman, for the first time in his career, looked confused.

'My son?'

'Yes, sir.'

'Here?'

'Yes, sir. I believe it's his first day.'

He checked his watch. It gave him the split-second he needed to regain the situation.

'Of course,' he said, looking up with a smile. 'It completely slipped my mind. Thank you, Sarah. I'll be right out.'

Sarah retreated, closing the door silently behind her. It was unusual for anything to slip Dwight Eagleman's mind. His mind was like fly-paper. So perhaps his son's first day hadn't slipped his mind at all – perhaps it was just too small to stick.

He gazed out over the city, wondering who he could palm his son off to for the day. The last thing he needed was a child to babysit while The Mac-Tonic™ Corporation faced its worst crisis in living memory.

Dwight Eagleman crossed the room and opened the office door. His son was sitting on the sleek red leather couch opposite Sarah's desk. He looked different: taller, but in that gangly way peculiar to growing boys. *How old is he now? Twelve? Fourteen?* Sarah would know – he'd check with her later. The boy looked more like his mother than his father: pretty rather than handsome, fair features instead of dark. Dwight Eagleman tried to remember the last time he'd seen his son and drew a blank. Christmas, one year, perhaps?

'That's a nice suit,' Dwight Eagleman said.

The boy smiled and looked down. It was a very nice suit. When he looked up, his father had taken a step closer and was holding out his hand.

'Welcome to Mac-Tonic™, son.'

The boy shook his father's hand and beamed, starstruck.

'Sarah,' Dwight Eagleman said, turning to the reception desk.

'Yes, Mr Eagleman?' Her smile, despite being the result of extensive cosmetic dentistry, and the cause of much childhood anxiety, looked amazingly authentic.

'My son will be starting in Research and Development. Could you call down and have one of them fetch him?'

'Certainly, sir.'

She picked up the phone and pressed a button.

The boy's face fell, his shoulders slumped. Dwight Eagleman saw his dismay and was pleased: the boy had ambitions above R&D. That was good. A thought crossed Dwight Eagleman's mind: *Why not throw him in at the deep end? There's nothing like a crisis to test someone's mettle: he'll either sink, or he'll swim.* There would be plenty of opportunities to spend time in other departments afterwards, when the storm had passed. So, for now, the boy would get his wish; Dwight Eagleman would tie him to the mast and steer into the tempest.

'On second thoughts, Sarah,' he said, 'I think perhaps he'd better come with me.'

Sarah replaced the phone in its cradle. Dwight Eagleman turned away from his son's look of pure gratitude and admiration and stepped through the frosted glass door. His son followed close behind.

'Sit there,' Dwight Eagleman said, pointing to a chair on the far side of an imposing circular table in the centre of the room. He had commissioned the table himself, shortly after the company's revenue hit one trillion dollars. It was made from a cross-section of General Sherman, the giant redwood that had been the largest living tree in the world until it had been felled to make a table. A rich varnish deepened the ruddiness of the wood and accentuated its two and a half thousand rings. The tree had been 275 feet tall; the tabletop was two inches thick.

The boy sat down and looked around the office. The wall opposite the floor-to-ceiling window showcased the company's history, with each point in the timeline illustrated by a Mac-Tonic™ bottle. In the beginning, they had been stubby, thick-glassed affairs, with swing-top seals and paper labels. But over the decades they had become curvy and elegant: a masterful synergy of beauty and utility. The final incarnation, at the very end of the row, was universally considered to be the perfect design. It fitted neatly into little hands and large alike, it had the perfect heft, and its undulating body was both wholesome and provocative: its nature changed with the beholder.

The boy wanted to ask a million questions about Mac-Tonic™ – about its history and its future – but no sooner had he opened his mouth than the rest of the board streamed into the room. Each man was dressed in an immaculate grey suit with a red Mac-Tonic™ badge pinned to his lapel. They seated themselves around the table and looked towards Dwight Eagleman. No one seemed to notice his son.

'Gentlemen,' Dwight Eagleman said, 'there has been a major incident.'

The circle of men sat up a little straighter. Dwight Eagleman stood at his usual spot, with his back to the New York skyline. It had the strange effect of throwing him slightly into shadow, so that his reflection on the polished table held more detail than his actual form.

'What kind of major incident?' asked Alexander Greenberg, who was so handsome he really should have been a movie star.

Dwight Eagleman rested his hands on the back of his chair. It was a deliberate gesture, as all of Dwight Eagleman's gestures were. Nothing was premeditated or rehearsed (the only thing he practised were facial expressions, to make sure he got them just right), but he always acted and spoke in a way that suggested he had read several pages further on than anyone else.

'You will all have noticed that two people who should be here are absent.'

The executives looked around. None of them had noticed anyone was absent. But sure enough, two plush leather seats were vacant. Somehow, they failed to spot the boy sitting between them.

'Funderburk and Hewitt are currently missing. Their planes did not reach their intended destinations.' Dwight Eagleman paused for a moment. 'It is not known what became of them, but both jets were last recorded somewhere over the Pacific Ocean.'

Dwight Eagleman allowed this information to sink in. He knew that each man needed a few seconds to get past the initial delight: with Funderburk and Hewitt out of the picture, their chances of one day taking Dwight Eagleman's place as CEO had just dramatically improved.

'I think we should observe two minutes' silence,' Dwight Eagleman said, 'as a mark of respect.'

The men bowed their heads. They made it to thirty-seven seconds before one of them spoke. Time is money, after all.

'What about the formula?' asked Martin DeWitt, his frown deepening.

Everyone stared at Dwight Eagleman. Now was the time to sit down, to take up his throne and join his subjects. Dwight Eagleman sat down.

'As you know,' he said, 'Funderburk and Hewitt each knew half the Mac-Tonic™ formula. Under normal circumstances, the death of a trustee would lead to a new board member learning his half of the recipe. But the death of both trustees creates a problem. The digital vault in which the two halves are stored requires two people – the CEO and the surviving trustee – to create a new secret keeper. My authorization alone is not enough.'

Each man took a slightly deeper breath. An almost imperceptible rustle of rich cotton and silk ran around the table.

'So what happens if they both kick the bucket?' asked Randy van de Velde, whose jowly cheeks were always flushed by his latest vexation.

Dwight Eagleman interlaced his fingers on the table. He was anchoring himself – securing his position. It also had the added benefit of making his hands resemble one giant, powerful fist.

'There is a physical copy of the formula in the company vault. It is an original document, handwritten by Horatio Macfarlane himself. There is also a vial of Mac-Tonic™ sealed inside the case, drawn from one of the original batches. I have already sent for the case from Madison's. When it arrives, I will share half the recipe each with two of you.'

There was an uncomfortable silence that Dwight Eagleman found entirely comfortable. Everyone at the table was unhappy with the prospect of one man knowing the whole formula – it was like entrusting the nuclear launch codes to a single person. But at the same time, no one wanted to be the one to raise an objection. After all, Dwight Eagleman hadn't disclosed which of them would become the new guardians of the recipe, and no one wanted to hurt their chances. Better to say nothing than something stupid.

It was while they were studiously avoiding each other's eyes that they became aware of the boy sitting at the table.

'Who's the kid?' Donnie Holland asked, light flashing off his slick side-parting as he turned to regard the boy.

The rest of the board observed him like an exotic pet. It seemed to break the tension.

'He's my son,' Dwight Eagleman said. 'Today is his first day.'

'Goddamn!' said Randy van de Velde. 'What a day to start! Just imagine: two planes going down on your first day. That's over one hundred million dollars knocked off the company's value like *that*.' Randy van de Velde clicked his fingers with an accomplished snap. 'Say, Dwight, you never said you had a cursed son.'

Dwight Eagleman smiled. He did not mind jokes about his son. His son had been out of the womb long enough to be responsible for his own failings and flaws. He could no longer affect his father's reputation.

'If I'd have known,' he said, 'I would have gotten him a job with Delixir™.'

The board had to laugh, so they laughed, even though the mention of their chief competitor made them bristle with rage and hunger for more dollars.

'This calls for a nickname,' Silvio Rizzuto said, a brilliant smile lighting up his face. 'The kid *needs* a nickname.'

This was exactly the kind of thing, as Head of International Marketing and Branding, that Lyle Funderburk would have excelled at. The men around the table seemed to realize this implicitly, and with it came an understanding that whoever successfully bestowed a nickname on Dwight Eagleman's son would be viewed as a worthy successor to Lyle Funderburk, and his claim to half the recipe. There was a good chance this would turn out to be one of Dwight Eagleman's legendary exercises in corporate selection. The board members fell silent and concentrated hard. The boy waited patiently for his new nickname.

'I've got it!' Alexander Greenberg said.

There was a controlled groan from the others, as though someone had just called 'house' in the most important game of bingo the world had ever known. They waited, praying to any god that would listen for Alexander Greenberg to say something stupid. Alexander Greenberg was Legal, a real rules and regulations guy; he had no business coming up with witty nicknames. Maybe he would land on his ass. The others could only hope.

'The Kennedy Kid,' Alexander Greenberg said.

He looked delighted with himself. The others looked perplexed.

Except for Dwight Eagleman, who smiled a smile that had become all too familiar during his triumphant tenure.

'I like it,' he said.

The others were still puzzled, but it would have been too painful to admit they needed an explanation. Luckily, Alexander Greenberg was always happy to elaborate on his achievements.

'Don't you see?' he said. 'It's a reference to the Kennedy family. Those guys are cursed as hell. They die in mysterious and tragic circumstances all the time. I mean, pretty much half the family tree has fallen out of the sky. And who can forget what happened to the President?'

There was a short silence. There were certain events that The Mac-Tonic™ Corporation refused to discuss.

Fortunately, a knock at the door interrupted them. It was Sarah.

'Good morning, gentlemen,' she said, before turning her attention to Dwight Eagleman. 'Sir, the package you sent for has arrived. Shall I send the courier in?'

Dwight Eagleman nodded. He did not stand up. He had an inkling that the person who walked through the door would be massive – probably ex-Special Forces – and he had no desire to be seen standing in the shadow of another man. To remain seated would be to retain power. Kings sit, servants stand.

Sure enough, a huge man dressed in a black suit and sunglasses stepped into the room. Handcuffed to his wrist was a steel briefcase. He stood awaiting further instructions.

'Over here,' Dwight Eagleman said.

The man nodded. He gave the impression – as he carefully positioned the briefcase in front of Dwight Eagleman – that in a previous life, most briefcases he'd handled had contained explosives or crucial enemy intelligence. He was very gentle, despite his strength. After the handcuffs had been unlocked he tucked them into his jacket pocket, nodded to the board and exited the room.

Dwight Eagleman stood. This was a monumental moment for The Mac-Tonic™ Corporation. For the first time since Horatio Macfarlane had brewed and bottled his new-fangled soda in a rickety shed almost a hundred and fifty years before, a single person was about to know the full recipe. It was knowledge most deemed too great for a single mind to contain. It was an immortal, supernatural thing. It was one of life's greatest mysteries. Does God exist? What's on the other side of a black hole? How do they get Mac-Tonic™ to taste so good?

And Dwight Eagleman approached that knowledge like a man stepping up to tee off at a charity golf tournament.

The briefcase was secured with two combination locks, a thumbprint scanner and voice recognition technology. Dwight Eagleman deftly scrolled to the right combination (his fingers working on each lock simultaneously), before pressing his thumbs against the small black ovals set into the case.

Then he spoke his own name.

A mechanism whirred as bolts retracted, eventually coming to a stop with a satisfying click.

Dwight Eagleman glanced up at the board before returning his attention to the case. Then, with a palm pressed on either side, he lifted the lid.

He stood for a moment, looking down. Half the board members expected some weird curse to strike him dead or melt the flesh from his bones, but nothing happened.

Instead, with a composure that generations of Mac-Tonic™ historians would fail to capture, he slowly rotated the briefcase to face the board.

'Gentlemen,' he said. 'I think we have a problem.'

The executives leaned closer. There was the gentle creak of leather, the whisper of rich cotton on silk. And then, as they say, the poop hit the propeller.

Because in the briefcase, where there should have been a small vial of Mac-Tonic™ and a piece of jaundiced paper, there was only an empty vial and a mess of melted grey sponge.

The vial had leaked.

Mac-Tonic™ could polish pennies, strip the enamel off teeth and remove even the most stubborn of skids from a toilet pan. A lot of acid was required to cut the sweetness – a hell of a lot – and so an aged piece of paper didn't really stand a chance.

Horatio Macfarlane's original recipe was destroyed.

The formula was lost.

It was a catastrophe the likes of which humanity had never encountered.

There was pandemonium in the boardroom, but amidst the uproar Dwight Eagleman was able to assess which of the men in front of him should be the next keepers of the formula, when this fiasco was eventually put right.

'This is a conspiracy!' exclaimed Randy van de Velde, pounding the table. 'And I demand to know who's at the bottom of it! I don't care what it takes, I want the guy responsible lynched. You hear me? Lynched!'

Needless to say, Randy van de Velde was not first pick to become a keeper of the formula.

Dwight Eagleman raised a hand. Silence fell over the room, but Randy van de Velde couldn't control himself.

'What the *hell* are we gonna do?'

He looked around the table. Blank faces stared back. It was Dwight Eagleman who responded. His voice was even and melodic and hypnotic.

'The first thing we are going to do is remain calm.'

'Calm?' said Randy van de Velde. '*Calm*? We've *lost* the formula! Without the formula, we can't make our product, and without our product, we can't make any money. And you're tryna tell me, the best goddamn salesman this company ever saw, to stay *calm*?'

Dwight Eagleman closed the briefcase. Its contents – or lack of contents – were only inflaming the situation. He placed the briefcase beside his chair, out of sight.

'Randy,' he said. 'You're embarrassing yourself.'

It didn't sound like an opinion coming from Dwight Eagleman; it sounded like an incontrovertible fact. Randy van de Velde bristled, but managed to hold his tongue.

'I know what you're saying is coming from a good place. You care about this company, and you're passionate about its success. We all are. This is the greatest company in the world. But right now we need to work out our next play, and the only way we'll be able to do that is if we remain calm.'

It was a solid team talk. Dwight Eagleman would have made an excellent basketball coach.

'So what is our next play?' asked Donnie Holland.

Dwight Eagleman clasped his hands behind his back and walked over to the wall of glass. The others watched in awe. It was a real honour to witness Dwight Eagleman deep in thought. It was like watching Michelangelo appraise a block of marble, like seeing Napoleon survey a battlefield. You knew that parameters were about to shift, that history was about to be made, that lives and life itself were about to change.

After a few minutes, he turned to address the room.

'Here's what we're going to do: at the end of the week, I'm going to hold a press conference with the world's media, and I'm going to tell them what's happened.'

Randy van de Velde looked incensed. 'You mean you're gonna tell those hacks *the truth*? Surely we need to keep this to ourselves, at least until we've managed to recover the recipe. There must be another copy – someone else who knows the formula!'

'Who?' asked Alexander Greenberg with undisguised contempt. 'Who else do you think knows the world's best-kept secret?'

'Well . . .' Randy van de Velde floundered for a few seconds, but then he found his feet. 'What about that creep Ritzendollar? He's been after our intellectual property since . . . well, since for ever!'

'*Ritzendollar*?' Martin DeWitt spat. 'Teddy Ritzendollar? Now why the hell would the CEO of Delixir™ know something about Mac-Tonic™ that we don't know ourselves?'

'Enough,' Dwight Eagleman said. 'Enough. There will be a press conference, and I will be telling the truth.'

'But think of the *share price*,' Randy van de Velde pleaded. 'What are the markets gonna make of a company that will run out of product in three weeks?'

'Two weeks, four days and six hours,' Dwight Eagleman said.

The room stopped.

'What did you just say?' Silvio Rizzuto asked.

'Two weeks, four days and six hours,' Dwight Eagleman repeated. 'That's how long it will be before the world runs out of Mac-Tonic™.'

The executives around the table looked decidedly unwell. A world without Mac-Tonic™ was inconceivable. Their logo was on the moon, after all. Randy van de Velde opened his mouth to speak, but could only gulp like a goldfish.

Dwight Eagleman returned to his seat at the table.

'When I tell the press what has happened, they will be convinced the whole things is an elaborate marketing stunt. Share prices will rise in anticipation of an exciting announcement. People will not be able to imagine a world in which Mac-Tonic™ is not available in every store, at every gas station, in every vending machine, and so they will carry on as normal. But soon places will start to sell out. This will lead to panic buying, which will increase the rate at which retailers run out of product. It will become apparent that Funderburk and Hewitt's planes did, in fact, disappear over the Pacific. Reports from halted production lines will confirm the situation. Our shares will tank.

'Two weeks, four days and six hours from now, there won't be a bottle of Mac-Tonic™ left on the shelves. Our other beverages won't generate enough revenue to support the company. Eventually, we will be forced to fold. It will be the end of The Mac-Tonic™ Corporation.'

This forecast was unimaginable. It was like asking the executives to envisage the moment immediately after their own deaths.

'Jeez, Dwight,' said Alexander Greenberg, after a while. 'This is bad. Real bad.'

Dwight Eagleman nodded.

'Our only hope is that the formula can be reverse-engineered from existing samples of Mac-Tonic™. Naturally, this is something we have always opposed as a company, but the time has come to throw all our weight behind this technology. I am confident that, with enough investment, a rapid breakthrough will be possible.'

'How rapid?' asked Martin DeWitt.

'Not rapid enough. There will be a spell when Mac-Tonic™ is unavailable – a kind of thirsty gap – but this will only serve to increase demand when it returns to the shelves.'

'And what if this reverse-engineering nonsense fails?' asked Randy van de Velde. 'What then?'

'I think the greater danger is that someone will withhold a breakthrough, for the purposes of ransoming. And so, as an additional measure, I think it would be prudent to contact the FBI, CIA, NSA and all other intelligence agencies and instruct them to suspend their ongoing investigations. We'll need to borrow their networks to monitor public communications.'

'Withhold the formula?' asked Randy van de Velde. 'Who would do something so heinous? So . . . unspeakable?'

There was much head shaking and sighing at the state of the world.

'We may be powerful,' said Dwight Eagleman. 'But that also makes us vulnerable. What do you think Delixir™ would pay to keep our formula from us?'

There was more head shaking. More sighing. The world really was a terrible place sometimes.

'So what should we do in the meantime,' asked Martin DeWitt, 'while we're waiting for this breakthrough?'

'We carry on,' Dwight Eagleman said. 'We persevere. We maintain our faith in the systems that have protected us and made us great.'

The others began to stir, as though some cue had been given that the meeting was over. Dwight Eagleman leaned forwards and pushed a button on the telephone.

'Sarah? Get the President on the line.'

'Yes, sir.'

The rest of the board exited the room. After a few seconds of waiting, a voice boomed from the speaker.

'Dwight!'

The Kennedy Kid listened as the President of the United States greeted his father like an old friend. So far he'd managed to keep the shock from his face, but this last revelation was too much: his father was friends with the most powerful man on Earth. The Kennedy Kid began to wonder what else he didn't know about his father.

'Mr President,' Dwight Eagleman said. 'I'm sorry to interrupt your golfing holiday, but something's come up. The time has come to return that favour . . .'

Mind Games

Queenie could never admit it to Ma, but those hippies had got her thinking. She'd grown so used to trash washing up and littering the shore that she'd stopped questioning it long ago; the beach had been a mess when they first moved in, and it had remained a mess ever since. Plastic bottles were the new seashells. And though she knew you were kind of responsible for your own trash, the thought of taking responsibility for someone else's had never occurred to her before.

And then there was the other big idea: that the world somehow belonged to her. It was exciting and sad and overwhelming, all at the same time. But it was the kind of idea that, once it got inside your head, was difficult to get out. Over the next few days it kept interrupting her thoughts like a commercial break, and she found herself actually *seeing* the trash, rather than seeing through it.

And so, after a week of mulling it over, Queenie took one of the garbage bags that Max and Linda had left behind and headed out to the water's edge.

Just as an experiment, she told herself. *Just to check how crazy those hippies really are.*

Besides, it wasn't like she had anywhere else to go, or anything better to do. Technically, Queenie and Chuckie were home-schooled. The authorities had only visited once and either decided that their educational needs were being met, or that raising a concern over their complete lack of education would mean having to go back – repeatedly – to that godforsaken shack owned by that godforsaken woman. Either way, the outcome was the same. The authorities left the de la Cruz family alone, and Ma left her children to entertain themselves.

As a result, Chuckie watched eight hours of TV a day, and he believed all kinds of nonsense. Chuckie was the kind of kid that fully believed if he ran off the edge of a cliff there would be a few seconds of frantic air-pedalling before he fell into the depths of the canyon below, only to appear in the next episode without a scratch. The kid watched eight hours of TV *every single day* and still hadn't worked out that commercial breaks are emergency exits. Instead, he watched the ads as though they meant something, as though they really spoke to him on some fundamental level. He was a salesman's dream.

Queenie, on the other hand, spent her time reading the extensive science fiction collection her uncle had left behind: yellowing, musty paperbacks written by authors with names like Geraldine F. Z. Lancelot, Andrei Zachariah Sokolov and Kilgore Trout. Unlike a lot of children her age, Queenie would have loved to attend school. Even though she feared the other kids would mock her for sounding like a hick, and for the farmer's tan that stopped just above her elbows, and for her shabby thrift store clothing, the opportunity to learn new things would have been worth the pain of being ostracized. Queenie knew there was a whole world to discover – she could see more of it from her back porch than most people – and it was a world that no number of TV channels could ever capture.

So maybe heading out with that sack wasn't just an idle experiment – maybe it was a small step into an unknown world.

Queenie reached the high-tide line and stopped. She looked around at the blanket of trash, and then looked back at the house; the last thing she needed was for Chuckie to spot her and scream the place down. But so long as the TV was on, Chuckie's whereabouts were almost entirely predictable.

Queenie turned back to the sand and, after a moment's pause, reached down for a Mac-Tonic™ bottle between her feet. She dropped it into the bag and waited. She wasn't sure what she was expecting to feel, but it certainly wasn't nothing. The hippies had looked happy, but she just felt a bit foolish. Undeterred, she stooped to pick up another bottle.

She might have imagined it, but there was something about the sound of the second bottle hitting the first at the bottom of the bag that lifted her spirits, like hearing the splash of coins when you drop a penny into a piggy bank. She tried another bottle, and found that she *did* feel better. She reached for another, and another, and another. Soon, the sack began to grow round and cumbersome. She dragged it along beside her, throwing in bottle after bottle, before eventually tying a knot at the top.

But then Queenie looked up, and it was like finding her piggy bank smashed to smithereens, the money gone. All she had managed to clear was a small patch of sand: the rest was still covered with trash, and more came surfing in with each lazy wave. That feeling of foolishness rushed back. The bulging bag beside her sat like an ugly testament to her stupidity.

She snatched it up, took a deep breath of acrid air and made to walk away. But as she turned she caught a glimpse of something riding the crest of a dirty wave. It was a Mac-Tonic™ bottle. And as the brown wave collapsed, flinging the bottle up the beach, she saw that there was something sealed inside it.

It looked like a roll of paper: a message in a bottle.

Queenie bent down and unscrewed the top. The coil of paper had uncurled slightly, and it wouldn't drop out. She poked a finger into the bottle, trying not to imagine whose lips might have touched it last, but she couldn't reach. She looked around for something to poke inside, but then stopped. Chuckie's voice came whining across the sand, angry and urgent, and it brought Queenie back to her senses.

What am I doing, groping around in other people's trash?

She trudged back to the house, shoved the bag of plastic bottles under the porch and tossed the other bottle in beside it. She'd worry about them later. Right now, she wanted to know what Chuckie was hollering about. But first, she needed a drink: she'd been looking at Mac-Tonic™ bottles for the last hour, and now she was thirsty. She stopped by the refrigerator on her way through the house and took a long gulp of Mac-Tonic™. The jittery nervousness she'd been barely conscious of subsided.

She carried her can through to the TV room where she found, unsurprisingly, Chuckie.

'Ma!' Chuckie hollered, the remote clutched in his fist. '*Ma!*'

'What?' she yelled back from another room. The walls were made of plywood, and her voice cut through them like a mitre saw.

'My show is off!' Chuckie replied.

'What?' Ma shouted.

Chuckie rolled his eyes, but somehow didn't take them from the screen.

'My. Show. Is. Off!'

'Watch something else then,' Ma said.

Chuckie flipped viciously from channel to channel, muttering under his breath.

'I can't!' he shouted.

'What?' Ma replied. She was still hollering from another room.

'I can't! There's some *man* on every channel!'

'What man? Is it the President?'

'How the hell am I supposed to know?'

'Watch your goddamn mouth!'

Chuckie was still channel hopping, despite its futility. Each station was exactly the same.

The sound of jingling and cartoonish explosions and squeaky-voiced cheering announced that Ma was on her way. She stopped behind the sagging couch, staring down at a phone that threw colourful light into her face, and played for at least another minute before looking up.

'That's not the President,' Ma said, scowling at Chuckie. 'That's Dwight Eagleman.'

On the screen, Dwight Eagleman stood behind a bank of multi-coloured microphones. He was getting ready to announce that in less than two weeks the world's supply of Mac-Tonic™ would dry up, but to look at him you would think he was about to declare another quarter of record growth. He smiled and made eye contact with just about every reporter crammed into the room. And then he leaned in.

Queenie dropped her can of Mac-Tonic™ when she found out about the missing formula, which was kind of ironic. It coughed a couple of fizzing mouthfuls across the floorboards before she could grab it again, but her hands shook with the horror of what she had just heard, and her breathing became shallow and raspy.

Chuckie kept flicking through the channels – there were just so many of them – but the news was on every single one.

'Queenie's going to freak out when she hears about this,' Chuckie said.

'I already heard!' Queenie said, recovering just enough to lambast her brother. 'I'm standing right here, you moron!'

There was a delay of a few seconds, as though Ma was coming to them live via satellite link, before she said, 'Mind your goddamn language.' Her voice was faraway, dreamy. It was like talking to someone who was hypnotized.

When she finally looked up from her phone, all she seemed to notice was the sticky patch of Mac-Tonic™ on the floor by Queenie's feet.

'What did you do that for? Don't just stand there, go and fetch the mop.'

Queenie left the room. She would have fetched a mop if they'd had one, but instead she had to settle for the broom that was propped on the porch. She made her way back to the TV room, poured some water on the stain and began scrubbing.

Chuckie had given up trying to find a different show. He eyed the remote control warily, like a loyal dog that had – after years of obedience – suddenly jumped up and bitten him. He left the TV on, even though he had no interest in the breaking news story. It was a habit.

Queenie scrubbed at the floor as though trying to scour all trace of the Mac-Tonic™ crisis out of existence. It just couldn't be true. But every time she looked up, there it was. The TV channel Chuckie had capitulated on showed zigzagging graphs and stock prices and men in suits taking it in turns to shout at one another. Chuckie lay on the couch, bored out of his mind. Ma stood in the doorway, her head bowed over her phone. She had been on her way somewhere to do something, but that was all forgotten now.

Chuckie suddenly sat up and twisted around to look at his sister. He grinned.

'What?' Queenie asked.

Chuckie kept grinning. It infuriated Queenie as only a sibling's smirk can.

'I said *what?*' Queenie stopped sweeping and clutched the shaft of the broom in both hands. 'What are you smiling at? Did you forget what a dunce you are or something?'

Chuckie's smile slipped for a moment, but then he remembered what he had to say.

'Sis, what are you going to do when all the Mac-Tonic™ is gone?'

It was like Chuckie had her heart in his hand, and he'd just given it a sickeningly painful squeeze. Queenie clenched her teeth against the rising nausea.

'It won't be *all* gone, dummy – there's no way they'd let that happen.'

Chuckie's smile widened.

'You're going to have to drink Delixir™.' He smacked his lips. '*Delectable, delicious Delixir™ – for those with taste!*'

Queenie's hands tightened around the broom handle.

'There's no way I'm drinking that stuff.'

'*A dozen a day keeps thirst at bay. Drink Delixir™!*'

'Chuckie, if you don't shut your trap I'm going to beat you to death with this broom, and that's a promise.'

'*Try Delixir™ – it's a de-light!*'

Queenie swung the broom, and Chuckie ducked just in time.

'Ma!' he shouted. 'Queenie's trying to kill me again!'

Queenie clambered over the back of the couch and raced after Chuckie. There was murder in her eyes, and Chuckie saw it.

'Ma!' he screamed again. 'Ma!'

He'd forgotten about the inevitable delay – the few seconds, or minutes, or hours it would take for his cries to penetrate the exploding fanfare of a new high score. By that time he'd be long dead, and Queenie would be headed for the state line, and no amount of scrubbing would remove his blood from the floorboards.

Queenie had him cornered, and she pushed the stiff bristles against his chest, pinning him to the wall.

'I'm never drinking that stuff, understand? Never!'

Queenie applied some extra force to the broom – she was surprisingly strong for someone so slight – and Chuckie let out a squeal. She'd always wondered how she'd kill Chuckie, and now she knew: she was going to squeeze the breath from him with a broom. The fact that the bristles were still wet with Mac-Tonic™ made the method all the more satisfying. She half expected him to start melting away like the Wicked Witch of the West.

But then the broom was yanked from her grasp. The force of it spun her around, so that she came face-to-face with Ma. Chuckie slumped to the floor, wheezing and coughing.

'What is wrong with you kids?' Ma screamed. 'I do everything for you – *everything!* – and this is the thanks I get! Your pa was a useless drunk but at least he knew how to keep you under control!'

Ma's eyes bulged with fury, her cheeks turned pink and her nostrils flared like a rampaging bull's. She raised the broom back over her shoulder and was about to swing it round when her phone emitted a tinkling sound – the kind you'd expect a sprinkling of fairy dust to make. She looked down to find that she'd just unlocked a new type of jewel and forgot all about the violence she'd been about to inflict.

Queenie stood in front of Ma, waiting to see whether she would snap out of her trance and bring the broom crashing down. But she'd slipped into the bottomless whirlpool of her phone. She may as well have not been in the room, or conscious, or even alive.

'Ma!' Chuckie said. He clambered to his feet and stood beside her, opposite Queenie. 'Ma, aren't you going to do something about *her*? She just tried to kill me!'

There was a few seconds' delay, and then Ma turned away, letting the broom clatter to the floor.

'Just get out of my sight, the pair of you!'

She walked from the room, transfixed by the shifting pattern of colours on her phone, like a cat watching an aquarium. There was a moment of truce as Queenie and Chuckie watched the space where their mother had been. Then they looked at each other, and at the broom on the floor.

It was closer to Chuckie.

He lunged for it.

Queenie took Ma's advice, and got the hell out.

Chuckie gave up on catching Queenie pretty soon after his feet hit the sand – there was a Chuckie-shaped impression in the couch cushions, after all – but Queenie didn't stop running. She scaled the dune that concealed her ramshackle house from the stretch of coast beyond, and made her way along the water's edge.

The beach here was scrubby and dull-looking, but it wasn't subject to the same conspiracy of factors that made Queenie's private beach a repository for discarded things. There were plastic bottles and wrappers and tangles of fishing-line tumbleweed, naturally, but they were spread out over a greater area, and that made the place seem less polluted. The thick cloud of smoke that spilled from the nearby incinerator was thinner too, and as Queenie made her way along the coast the sun began to break through with growing intensity.

When it was too hot to run, Queenie slowed to a walk. She kicked a Mac-Tonic™ bottle as hard as she could.

Typical! she thought. *Why couldn't it have been Delixir™ instead? The one thing I can't live without, and they go and lose the recipe in the middle of the Pacific Ocean!*

She moved up the beach, glancing back every now and then to check that Chuckie wasn't sneaking up to assassinate her, and reached a sidewalk that was dusty with sand.

There was a row of derelict storefronts on the opposite side of the road, facing the ocean. Inside each unit were dusty counters and piles of cardboard boxes and shelves that had fallen from their pegs. The signs above each window revealed what the units had once been – The Surf Shop, The Ice Cream Shack, Yolanda's Bakery, North Nitch Knick-knacks – but it must have been a decade or more since any dollars had changed hands on the premises.

Queenie crossed the road and kept walking until she came to a huge expanse of asphalt. She cut across it, heading towards a store that looked more like a factory or a giant cattle shed than a place to buy food. The asphalt was hot beneath her flip-flops. It took her a while to reach the entrance; the car park was about the size of five football fields.

The doors slid open, and Queenie stepped into a vast, air-conditioned hangar. She immediately felt both calm and anxious. On the one hand, there was soft, soporific music drifting down from the steel rafters – the kind of music that gets played in elevators – that relaxed her. But then there was the relentless beeping of goods being rung up, the tinkle of coins and the whisper of dollars, the battering of cash registers popping open, the drone of inane small talk between strangers. And then there was the *choice*: the endless aisles of things to buy. There were probably people who had been wandering the store since the day it opened. It made her brain ache.

Queenie walked along the front of the store as quickly as she could. Her plan was to buy as much Mac-Tonic™ as she could with the money in her pocket – just in case there was a shortage – and get out as soon as possible. The Mac-Tonic™ was always located in the farthest corner of a store: it meant that every customer had to run the gauntlet of special offers and promotions to reach the thing they really wanted. It had the added benefit of making people feel like they'd achieved something when they finally reached the soda aisle. It was a good feeling, and the soda felt like a reward.

It was a mind game. It was all about mind games.

Queenie heard the commotion before she saw what was causing it. She turned into the soda aisle and found a huddle of angry customers surrounding a bewildered store worker. He had his back to a cage trolley that was half full of Mac-Tonic™ crates. The store manager stood next to him with his hands raised.

'Hey!' a woman in sunglasses shouted. She swung her handbag at the manager. 'Hey! You can't do this! We have human rights!'

'Yeah!' said a big man in a stained vest. 'This isn't right! It's un-American!'

'Please,' said the shop manager. 'If everyone could just stay calm. This is merely a temporary measure until—'

'You're damn right it's a temporary measure,' said the big man, jabbing a finger into the manager's chest, 'because you're going to get your boy here to put those crates back on the shelf, where they belong.'

Queenie looked along the aisle. The Mac-Tonic™ was kept on one side, the Delixir™ was kept on the other. It was store policy. It may have even been domestic and foreign policy, for all she knew. But today, the Mac-Tonic™ side was half empty. As she watched the mob, someone else in a store uniform dragged another cage trolley to the shelves and started removing crates of Mac-Tonic™.

'Now there's another one!' wailed an elderly lady.

'This isn't my decision!' the manager protested. 'It has come from higher up, way above my pay grade.'

'You're on your way to a hiding,' an old man in a trilby hat and braces proclaimed. 'A damn good hiding.' He brandished his walking stick as though he would be the one to administer it.

'Look,' the manager said. His hands were still raised. 'There's nothing to stop you buying items that are still on the shelves. There are plenty of Mac-Tonic™ products for sale at the far end of the aisle.'

'Were you dropped on your head as a baby or something?' the big man asked. 'All that's left down there are cans and plastic bottles, and everyone knows Mac-Tonic™ tastes best from a *glass* bottle.'

It was true. Mac-Tonic™ did taste best from a glass bottle. There were many noises of agreement from the mob.

The manager finally lost his patience and said something that, given the situation, was wholly inadvisable.

'There's a whole *wall* of Delixir™ in glass bottles right behind you! Drink some of those!'

It was unforgivable. There was a collective gasp. The old lady fainted. The trolley boys looked at their manager as though he had just confessed to multiple homicides. The manager lifted a trembling hand to his mouth.

'Oh, God,' he muttered. He gripped his head between his hands. 'Oh, God.'

But it was no good. He had committed the cardinal sin of selling stuff. He had suggested that two products that were remarkably alike were, in fact, remarkably alike. It was like a magician talking his audience through the secrets of a magic trick as he performed it. The mob was dumbstruck. They clung to reality even as it crumbled around them. They were dazed, and then they were confused, and then they got mad.

Queenie had witnessed enough trailer park altercations to know she was looking at a felony in the making. She grabbed a crate of Mac-Tonic™ cans from the shelf and ran. When she reached the end of the aisle, she looked back. It was obvious that the manager was on the floor, but it wasn't clear who was making him whimper.

Queenie put her Mac-Tonic™ down at the checkout, shoved her money at the cashier and snatched the crate up again.

'You might want to call 911,' she said.

There was a crash of glass, and shrieking, and then the shooting started.

Queenie ran and did not look back.

Joyride to Armageddon

The board was back around General Sherman, discussing the fate of the world. It had been ten days since the executives found themselves without a formula, and so far no breakthrough in the reverse-engineering process had come. The greatest minds from various scientific fields – medicine, pharmaceuticals, water purification, aeronautical engineering, toxicology, forensic criminology – had slammed the brakes on their research to join the quest. Mac-Tonic™ had allocated millions of dollars to the enterprise. They were willing to fund anyone who restored the formula.

In addition to the eggheads with their test tubes and Petri dishes and doctorate certificates hanging on the wall, millions of people were praying to a whole smorgasbord of deities, so all the bases were covered.

'Any news on the formula?' Martin DeWitt asked.

The others around the table avoided making eye contact with Dwight Eagleman; only the Kennedy Kid looked right at him.

'No,' Dwight Eagleman said. He didn't sound happy or sad about the fact. To him, it just seemed to be an answer to a question.

'Say,' said Randy van de Velde, sitting back in his chair and stroking his tie between two fingers. 'What happens when the formula *is* deduced?'

All eyes turned to him. There was a smile in his voice that he was fighting hard to keep from his face. Dwight Eagleman appraised him coolly. He knew what the question was really about, but he wouldn't be the one to raise the subject.

Randy van de Velde sat forwards and clasped his hands on the gleaming redwood. 'What I mean is, what happens to *the discoverer* of the formula? Are we really gonna have some outsider – some *scientist* – knowing a company secret like that? Free to tell whoever he wants?' He looked around the room, his eyes wide.

It was a good point. The executives all seemed to contemplate the horror of such a scenario for a few seconds before stealing a glance at their leader. Dwight Eagleman looked at Randy van de Velde. He did not blink.

'Would you like to suggest a solution?' he asked.

It was evident, from Randy van de Velde's expression and demeanour, that he had considered this problem long and hard – for a minimum of at least seven minutes. There were clearly many solutions available to them. Randy van de Velde was a keen amateur historian; as a result, he knew of a million ways to make people disappear once they'd served their purpose. His favourite was the one about the clockmaker who had his eyes put out after finishing the astronomical clock in Prague, so that he couldn't make anything as beautiful ever again. He liked how things were done back in the olden days: efficient, no-nonsense, businesslike. He belonged there, in the past. He felt at home.

But before he had a chance to share his medieval vision, someone else spoke up.

'We could offer a cash reward,' the Kennedy Kid said, 'and whoever rediscovers the recipe could receive a lifetime's supply of Mac-Tonic™.'

The executives flinched as one; they'd all completely forgotten about the Kennedy Kid.

Randy van de Velde scowled. 'Rewards make people complacent and greedy. It wouldn't be long before they were looking to sell the recipe to the highest bidder. The person in question would need to be removed from public life. Permanently.'

There were nods of approval. The Kennedy Kid looked to his father for some kind of support, but Dwight Eagleman was unreadable.

'Thank you, Randy,' he said. 'We will cross that bridge when we come to it.'

The Kennedy Kid slumped back in his chair. He'd been shadowing these board meetings for over a week now, trying to learn the ways of the magnate, trying to make his father proud. But every suggestion he made was either shot down or ignored. It was like everyone else spoke a different language.

And what does it actually mean to permanently remove someone from public life? he wondered. His brain flitted from one possibility to another, but each scenario made his scalp prickle. He must have misunderstood Randy van de Velde's meaning.

'It would be good to hear how some of our ongoing projects are progressing,' Dwight Eagleman said. 'Alexander?'

'Right,' said Alexander Greenberg, sitting forwards and leafing through a bound dossier on the tabletop.

'This is a report produced by Consumer Group International on the subject of waste and pollution.'

'Not this again,' Randy van de Velde said. 'When are people gonna give up talking about this stuff?' He shook his head and sat back, like a disgruntled defendant being read a list of his crimes. 'Go on, go ahead. Let's get it over with.'

'As part of the study, CGI conducted some tests on the Great Pacific Garbage Patch—'

'The what?' asked Randy van de Velde.

'The Great Pacific Garbage Patch.'

'And what in the hell is the Great Pacific Garbage Patch?'

There was a pause. 'It's a patch of garbage,' Alexander Greenberg said. 'In the Pacific Ocean.'

Randy van de Velde snorted. Alexander Greenberg carried on.

'According to this report, it's about three times the size of France.'

'Why don't they use a measure people can understand?' Randy van de Velde asked. 'Who knows how big a place France really is? Why can't they use football fields instead?'

'Well, the report offers an alternative scale. The Patch is about twice the size of Texas.'

Randy van de Velde whistled. 'Hoooo-eeeee! Hot damn, that's big! No wonder they don't use football fields. And who knew three Frances add up to two Texases? Europe must be a tiny place. Sorry, Al, you go right ahead with your little report.'

'As I said, they took some samples for analysis and, well . . .'

There was a bristling pause as the executives readied themselves for the bad news.

'How bad is it?' Donnie Holland asked.

'Pretty bad,' said Alexander Greenberg. 'From the samples they collected, they were able to estimate how much of that trash comes from Mac-Tonic™ products.' He hesitated, like a doctor on the brink of announcing a bleak diagnosis. 'It's forty-two per cent.'

A muttering, hissing, tutting sound rippled around the table.

'Forty-two per cent!' Randy van de Velde shouted. 'Forty-two per cent!'

'Oh, hell,' said Martin DeWitt. 'That's terrible. Did we have a target for this, Dwight? Did we hit our target?'

Dwight Eagleman shook his head. 'This is an initial report, so no target was set. But I think our market share means we should be striving for at least fifty-one per cent of that Patch.'

The Kennedy Kid was confused. *They want to be responsible for more trash in the ocean?* Like everything else that occurred in the boardroom, it didn't make sense.

'I agree,' said Alexander Greenberg. 'We need to be the leader in everything we do, including pollution. Speaking of which, I have another report here on global warming.'

If there were two words that really riled Randy van de Velde – right after 'Drink Delixir™' – they were 'global warming'.

'Not another one!' he said. 'I thought the President had sorted this already?' He looked like a man who could not – just *could not* – believe what he was hearing. 'Go on, then. I'm all ears!'

'The report states that global temperatures are rising, and the authors make a pretty compelling case for how big business is the driving force. Mac-Tonic™ was named specifically, but unfortunately so was Delixir™. However, the take-home message is that global temperatures are on the rise, and so long as we keep on doing what we're doing they'll keep on rising.'

'I'm still not convinced it's even a real thing,' Randy van de Velde muttered.

'It's real,' Dwight Eagleman said, 'and it's one of the greatest sales opportunities the world has ever known.'

The Kennedy Kid had always thought 'jaw-dropping' was just an expression, but suddenly he found himself with his mouth hanging open in disbelief. He snapped it shut before anybody noticed.

They think climate change is a business opportunity?

Randy van de Velde raised a sceptical eyebrow. 'How so?'

Dwight Eagleman examined the cuticles of his left hand before responding. 'Just think about it. We are in the business of refreshment. Get someone to think of summertime and it won't be long before they start thirsting for an ice-cold Mac-Tonic™. The hotter it gets, the greater the need for refreshment. The greater the need for refreshment, the greater our demand. We should be doing everything in our power to ensure that this planet gets as hot as possible.'

Dwight Eagleman spoke about planet Earth as though he knew of a dozen other habitable worlds. It was an invaluable trait: it meant there was no venture too risky; no action too rash; no project too ambitious for the universe to accommodate, even if good ol' Mother Earth would combust under the strain.

'Agreed,' said Alexander Greenberg.

Now the Kennedy Kid really had lost the trail of breadcrumbs. *They want the planet to get hotter . . . just to sell more bottles of Mac-Tonic™?* He knew people were crazy for the stuff, but surely it wasn't worth risking the planet for?

He had to speak up, even though everyone else seemed to be nodding in agreement.

'Maybe it's not such a good idea.' There was a disapproving silence, but the Kennedy Kid persevered. 'Some regions will get colder, you know, so we'll end up losing sales.'

'Can't they make their minds up?' Randy van de Velde said. 'I thought it was supposed to be global *warming*.'

'I believe it's quite a complicated process,' the Kennedy Kid said.

Randy van de Velde glowered. 'I thought kids were supposed to be seen and not heard. You ever hear that expression?'

The Kennedy Kid held Randy van de Velde's stare, but he also held his tongue. He might have little influence in these meetings, but he'd have even less if they kicked him out. And without him, there wouldn't be anyone trying to stop this joyride to Armageddon.

'Cold spots are good news, anyway,' said Silvio Rizzuto. 'Over in R&D, we're busy perfecting a selection of hot beverages.' The rest of the board nodded in mild appreciation. 'They taste good,' Silvio Rizzuto added.

'That's great to hear,' said Alexander Greenberg. 'Another upside of global warming is that there will be a sharp rise in the occurrence and duration of droughts, as well as the general desertification of land mass. It's expected that tens of millions of people will see their access to drinking water disappear. Naturally this is a huge potential market, and it's a market we need to fully exploit. There's real scope for an entire customer base that exclusively drinks Mac-Tonic™ beverages, simply because they don't have access to anything else.'

'In a hot and arid future,' Dwight Eagleman said, 'it needs to be our product that quenches this parched planet.'

A solemn silence settled around the table. There was appetite and opportunity for an 'amen', but nobody wanted The Mac-Tonic™ Corporation to turn into some kind of mad cult. In the eyes of the Kennedy Kid, they were already there.

'Randy,' Dwight Eagleman said. 'How was your trip to Italy?'

'Oh, don't get me started on them Italians.' He hit the 'I' like an iceberg. 'No offence, Silvio.'

Silvio Rizzuto frowned. 'I'm not Italian.'

Randy van de Velde cast a disbelieving glance in Silvio Rizzuto's direction. He adjusted himself in his chair, shook his head and returned his attention to the others.

'You know, I had a lunch meeting that lasted for three hours. *Three. Hours.* And we didn't even discuss one item of business. Every time I tried to bring up the Sistine Chapel they waved it off and called for more wine. So I bided my time, thinking that as soon as lunch was done we'd get down to it. And d'you know what? After lunch they all go off for a sleep. *In the middle of the afternoon.* A nap! Can you believe it? I mean, don't they realize that time is money?'

There was much head shaking at the state of the world.

'Anyways, we finally managed to talk business and . . .' Randy van de Velde paused to heighten the tension, then brought his palm down on to the table with a resounding slap. His eyes were wild, like a frenzied animal's. 'They agreed to it all!'

A brief episode of whooping and hollering and fist pumping broke out. Martin DeWitt reached over and slapped Randy van de Velde on the back.

'I knew you had good news for us,' Martin DeWitt said. 'You had that tell-tale twinkle in your eye.'

'Guilty as charged!' Randy van de Velde yelled. 'You wanna see what it's gonna look like?'

Of course, everybody did. It was arguably the most significant feat of cultural integration since Lady Liberty acquired her new accessory. Randy sprang from his chair like a man half his age and stepped out into the lobby. He was back a moment later with a long plastic tube tucked under his arm. He prised the lid off, slid out a roll of paper and let it unfurl across the table. The sheet was specially weighted at its corners so that it didn't curl up on itself, and the members of the board leaned in for a closer look.

The entirety of the sheet was filled with a reproduction of Michelangelo's *The Creation of Adam*, ceiling cracks and all. In the centre of the painting, someone had skilfully inserted a bottle of Mac-Tonic™ into Adam's outstretched hand, and a waiting glass into God's.

'Isn't it perfect?' Randy van de Velde asked. He sounded smitten. 'We're thinking of renaming it *The Recreation of Adam*. The original painting is over five hundred years old, so it'll be mighty delicate work, but they're gonna get their finest conservator to add the improvements. Plus, they've agreed to place a Mac-Tonic™ vending machine in each corner of the Sistine Chapel, as well as throughout the Vatican Museums that lead to it.'

The rest of the board gazed upon the fresco, and they saw that it was good. Too good, in fact. All of them regarded Randy van de Velde as a maverick, a go-getter, and a damn fine salesman, but none of them had ever viewed him as a serious contender for the position of CEO. He was too unpredictable, too wild, too much. But with a coup like this under his belt, who knew?

With perfect synchronicity, each member of the board turned their attention from the god in the fresco to the god in the room.

It was bad news; Dwight Eagleman was not an easy man to impress. But Dwight Eagleman looked impressed.

It was time to go in for a professional foul.

'And what about the trip to Delhi?' Donnie Holland asked.

Randy van de Velde's blissful expression fell from his face. He waved his hand dismissively. 'They won't take any more volume.'

Dwight Eagleman's eyes narrowed. Randy van de Velde's moment in the sun had passed.

'Come on, Randy,' Martin DeWitt said. 'There are over a billion people in India, and we're shipping less to them than the goddamn Brits!'

'And you think you could do a better job?' Randy van de Velde asked. 'I told you, they won't take another drop – not from me, and certainly not from you.'

'But that territory is a goddamn godsend!' Silvio Rizzuto said, jumping to his feet. They were all piling in now, like big cats digging their claws into the hide of a buffalo: slowing it down, tiring it out, making it bleed.

'You really think so?' said Randy van de Velde. 'Well, seeing as you're the expert in these matters, why don't you enlighten me?'

Randy van de Velde sat back in his chair and crossed his arms. He was asking the predators to demonstrate just how sharp their claws were, when he really should have been bucking and stamping and goring great big holes in their flanks.

'Look at this masterpiece,' Silvio Rizzuto said, pointing to *The Recreation of Adam* on the table between them. 'What do you notice about God's arms?'

'What?' Randy van de Velde hauled himself forwards and looked at God. His arms were muscular and perfectly proportioned, and the one that wasn't reaching out for an ice-cold glass of Mac-Tonic™ was wrapped around a woman.

'What am I looking for here?' he asked.

Silvio Rizzuto rolled his eyes. 'How many arms does God have?'

'What in the world are you talking about, boy?'

'It's a simple question, Randy. How many arms does he have?'

'Two.' Randy van de Velde had an overwhelming urge to check the number of divine limbs in the painting, but he held Silvio Rizzuto's stare.

'That's right. Now tell us what the most popular religion in India is.'

Randy van de Velde was convinced that the only people who knew the answer to that question were the Indians themselves, just like the only people who knew how big France was were the French, but he still felt foolish. What if the others did know somehow?

'It's Hinduism,' the Kennedy Kid mumbled, miserably. He seemed to be the only one who thought *The Recreation of Adam* was a monstrosity.

'It's Hinduism,' Silvio Rizzuto said, pretending not to have heard the Kennedy Kid. He was still standing, but he had lowered his voice, like a teacher who had regained control of a boisterous classroom. 'Would you like to guess how many gods and goddesses there are in the Hindu faith, Randy?'

Randy van de Velde suddenly saw where this line of questioning was headed, and it ended with vultures picking a buffalo carcass clean. *The Recreation of Adam* had somehow become a giant sixteenth-century poster advertising his failure to sell better in India. It belonged in Revelation, not Genesis.

'Lots,' he said, through clenched teeth.

'That's right. Too many to count. And do you know what a common feature of Hindu deities is?'

Randy van de Velde refused to answer. (He didn't actually know the answer, but he refused to go willingly to the place of his death. Silvio Rizzuto and the others would have to drag him.)

'They have lots of arms,' Silvio Rizzuto said. 'Brahma, Vishnu, Ganesh.' He held up four fingers. 'Four arms each. Hell, Durga has *eight*! So while this masterpiece may impress some people, I think what the rest of us would like to know is why you aren't plying the Hindu gods with bottles of Mac-Tonic™ too? Maybe if the good people of India had some divine inspiration, our sales there might improve.'

Randy van de Velde held Silvio Rizzuto's merciless gaze for as long as he could, but he couldn't hold it for ever. He was blowing hard, and bleeding freely, and he knew it. Eventually he slumped to his knees, and strong jaws clamped around his throat, and he gave a final bleat before succumbing to the hunt.

The Kennedy Kid watched it all, horror-struck.

The Great Thirst

The world ran out of Mac-Tonic™; the Great Thirst began.

Queenie was down to her last three cans, and she was determined not to drink them until the recipe had been found. But it was tough. Gruelling, in fact. The caffeine withdrawal made her tired and anxious and irritable.

And then there was the sugar withdrawal.

At first, she was simply confused. And then her cravings grew so intense that she began searching out anything sweet which – hers being an American household – was like looking for sand in the desert. But the snacks and treats filled her up before she could get an adequate sugar hit. She was used to liquid sugar that passed right through and made space for more. It was a wretched predicament. She even considered drinking the Delixir™ that Chuckie guzzled all day long.

That was when she suspected she was losing her mind.

Her madness was confirmed when she found herself hugging Chuckie and crying uncontrollably. She couldn't sleep. She felt depressed. She even ventured to the supermarket where the shooting had occurred in a desperate quest to find more supplies of Mac-Tonic™, but it was pandemonium. It was like something out of the Bible. It was like Black Friday.

Every day for the past few weeks there had been news reports of street brawls and riots and looting. One station had even taken to recording fatalities inspired by the shortage – murders of passion, death by misadventure, dehydration – with a Mac-Tonic™ Death-o-Meter in the corner of the screen that crept up by a dozen or so every hour.

Chuckie was in his element. TV had never been so good. And to top it all, he could sit back with a tall glass of Delixir™ and really savour it. The fact that his sister was close to insanity made his ice-cold Delixir™ even sweeter. Ma, in her desperation, had started drinking Delixir™ too, which meant there was even more of it in the refrigerator. It was almost too good to be true.

Queenie came into the TV room to find Chuckie guzzling Delixir™ and gobbling up the latest news item. A prestigious New York auction house was taking bids on a dozen crates of Mac-Tonic™ in glass bottles that some shrewd entrepreneur had somehow kept by. There was a live feed to the crowded auction room, although the crates of Mac-Tonic™, for obvious reasons, had been kept at a secure location. As with the sale of expensive artwork, the bidders were represented by proxies, so as to preserve their anonymity.

When Queenie entered the room, the bidding was at $300,000. By the time she left, five minutes later, it was at $1.5 million and still climbing. Those who had been outbid were starting to make a scene. It was highly embarrassing and highly understandable. You know things are really bad when the rich people start to panic.

Queenie had to get out. She needed a drink of Mac-Tonic™. Her head felt like it was trapped in a car crusher. It wouldn't be so bad if everyone stopped talking about it, but you couldn't find a network willing to show anything else. Queenie barged out on to the back porch, shoving the door so hard it swung and clattered into the peeling boards of the house and, by some miracle, didn't drop off its hinges. She hurried down the sagging steps and crawled beneath the porch to where her secret stash was hidden. There was no chance of Chuckie drinking them, but there was every chance that if he found the cans he would hide them for the purposes of extortion, or simply to watch his sister fall apart. Sometimes, on the nights she managed to get some sleep, Queenie dreamed that Chuckie had found her stash and was standing at the ocean's edge, gleefully pouring the last of her Mac-Tonic™ into the brown water. When she woke in a cold sweat, she had to venture outside to check the cans were still safe.

Queenie snapped the ring pull on the nearest can and took thirsty gulps that stung her nostrils and made her eyes water. It wasn't as cold as it should have been, but the sweet, fizzing soda began firing neurons and releasing brain chemicals the moment it touched her tongue. She felt like a werewolf watching the full moon disappear behind a thick bank of clouds. There was suddenly a glimpse of normality, of sanity. She sat back against one of the porch supports and drank her can of Mac-Tonic™ in the gloom.

At one point she heard Chuckie yell, 'Hey, Queenie, some dumbass ended up paying twelve million dollars for those lousy crates of Mac-Tonic™! That's like . . .' There was a long pause. '. . . a million dollars a crate! Some people are so goddamn stupid!'

'Watch your goddamn mouth!' Ma hollered. A tinkling cascade of jewels trickled through the floorboards shortly afterwards. She must have hit a new high score. The woman was unstoppable.

Queenie let the empty can fall on to the sand between her feet and rested her head on her knees. It had taken the edge off, but already the itch was creeping across her body like a forest of thorns in a fairy tale. She thought about making a cup of coffee. She hated coffee, but with six teaspoons of sugar mixed in, it did similar things to her brain chemistry as Mac-Tonic™. Or maybe she should just drink another can now? They weren't going to last for ever. If there was one thing TV had taught her, it was that there is nothing to be gained from self-discipline or delayed gratification.

It was all so futile. Even if she managed to suppress her cravings, it would only be for a matter of hours – maybe days. She was trapped, and no amount of self-denial or avoidance or wishful thinking would make the tiniest bit of difference: at some point, she would end up drinking the last Mac-Tonic™ she was ever likely to taste.

She lifted her head from her knees and crawled out of her sanctuary. A pang of guilt shot through her as she passed the bag of plastic bottles she'd collected from the shore all those weeks ago. She'd meant to carry on, to go out the next day and pick up more, but then the Mac-Tonic™ crisis – with all its maddening cravings – had taken over everything.

Queenie was about to emerge from beneath the porch when something caught her eye and made her stop. Lying next to the bag of trash was the Mac-Tonic™ bottle with the message inside. The Great Thirst had made her forget all about that, too, but now her curiosity was piqued, her befuddled mind suddenly focused.

She grabbed the bottle and carried it to her bedroom. Using a pen, she teased the roll of paper towards the neck of the bottle and out through its mouth. As soon as there was enough sticking out, she pinched it between her finger and thumb and extracted it.

It was the wrap from the Mac-Tonic™ bottle. On one side was the iconic looping logo and a small box of abridged ingredients, and on the other was, well, another list of ingredients, carved into the paper with what looked like a piece of charcoal, or a spent match. Even still, it was clear that two different people had contributed to the list.

Queenie tilted it to the dim light and read:

And at the bottom, squeezed under the last item, were two words:

SEND HELP!

Queenie's heart was suddenly thumping at the back of her throat. She held the paper between trembling fingers, transfixed. She was thinking inconceivable thoughts. It was just a piece of trash. She'd been deprived of Mac-Tonic™ for too long, and now she was hallucinating. But there it was, in her hand. She could feel the plasticized label beginning to sweat in her palm as the possibilities, the responsibilities, the repercussions, began to crowd around her.

This was it – the recipe. The missing formula. She had found it!

Queenie stood in her dingy bedroom, looking out at the litter-strewn Pacific Ocean. She was the only person in the world who knew how to make Mac-Tonic™.

For a few seconds, at least.

'What's that?' Chuckie asked.

Queenie whipped round and scowled at Chuckie.

'None of your damn business!' she said. 'What are you even doing in here? Is the TV broken or something?'

'I came to tell you that those crates of Mac-Tonic™ turned out to be a scam. Some bozo paid twelve million dollars for a dozen crates of store soda. Imagine that, huh?'

His eyes never left the label that was clutched in Queenie's hand.

'Well, you've told me, so now you can go away.'

But Chuckie didn't move.

'What is it?' he asked.

'I told you,' Queenie said. 'None of your damn business.'

'If it's nothing,' Chuckie said, taking a step forwards, 'you won't mind if I take a look.'

He lunged at Queenie, but she saw it coming and caught him off-balance, driving him back into the hallway with all her strength. She slammed the door shut and leaned her weight against it. Chuckie began hammering with his fist.

'Open up!' he shouted. 'Open up right now or I'll bust the damn door.'

'What the hell are you kids doing now?' Ma said. Queenie had never been so pleased to hear her mother's voice.

'Chuckie won't leave me alone!'

The floorboards groaned as Ma approached the bedroom door. A cartoon explosion was followed by a cheering sound, like garden gnomes on helium.

'Ma!' Chuckie shouted, even though she must have been standing right next to him. 'Queenie's got something she isn't supposed to have, and she won't give it up!'

'Queenie,' Ma said. 'You come out right this instant and hand it over.'

'No, Ma, please. It's nothing. It's just a piece of trash.'

'I won't ask again,' Ma said.

'It looked like drugs,' Chuckie mumbled apologetically. 'Maybe it was those hippies . . .'

'Drugs!' Ma said. 'I knew we never should have moved to California!'

'It's not drugs!' Queenie said. 'Chuckie, shut your goddamn trap!'

'Queenie, if you don't hand over those drugs right now I'm gonna come in there and give you such a hiding you'll *need* drugs just to sit down!'

'Ma! It's not drugs!'

'Queenie, don't make me knock down this door!'

'Do it, Ma!' Chuckie said.

Queenie imagined Ma throwing her 300-pound frame into the door. It would be like being hit by a cannonball. The door would splinter into a thousand pieces. Queenie would be crushed.

'Fine!' Queenie shouted. 'Fine! I'll tell you what it is, but I'm not opening the door.'

There was a grudging silence. Queenie took a deep breath and looked down at the label in her hand.

'It's the Mac-Tonic™ formula, all right? It washed up in a bottle—'

Total Blackout

'Brenda, did you hear that?'

Brenda pulled off her headphones and hung them around her neck.

'Yep,' she said, flicking a switch beside her monitor. 'Recording.'

'Could be nothing,' Cameron said, adjusting his own headphones.

'And it could be something,' Brenda replied. She checked the clock mounted above the colossal screen at the front of the room, scribbled something on a notepad and repositioned her headphones over her ears.

For a few moments they listened without saying anything. Brenda was chewing a piece of peppermint-flavoured gum. Cameron glanced over at her.

'They sound Midwestern, but the phone's GPS is placing them out on the California coast. Vacation, you think?'

'Uh-huh,' Brenda said. She enlarged a map on her monitor. 'Town called North Nitch. Hardly anything on the database – must either be an undiscovered gem or a real dive. Apparently there was an M-T™-related multiple homicide there a few weeks ago, so I'm guessing the latter. Could be significant, though?'

Cameron arched his eyebrows. 'Find me a town that hasn't had an M-T™-related multiple homicide in the past few weeks.'

'Good point.' They listened some more. Brenda stopped chewing and frowned. 'What *is* that noise?'

'Sounds like one of those never-ending puzzle games. Annoying, huh?'

'Think we can mute it? I'm struggling to hear what the girl is saying. Sounds like they're having the conversation through a door.'

'Give me one second,' Cameron said. He typed a long line of code into his keyboard. 'I'll increase the microphone sensitivity too.'

'Roger that.'

Brenda glanced around while she waited for Cameron to work his magic. Rows of long desks stretched from one side of the vast room to the other. At regular intervals, men and women sat hunched over keyboards and monitors, watching and listening and logging. At the front of the space, a screen the size of a basketball court displayed a map of the USA, criss-crossed with golden threads of light like the retinal scars left by fireworks. There were small green dots scattered across the map denoting conversations of interest, concentric circles radiating from each one, like ripples spreading across a tranquil pond.

Brenda arched her back and rolled her head from side to side. Her eyes ached but she couldn't complain – this assignment wasn't so bad. It was better than eavesdropping on terrorists, in any case, which was what everyone – Brenda and Cameron included – had been doing up until the Mac-Tonic™ formula went AWOL.

'OK,' Cameron said. 'That should make things easier. Let's hope the conversation doesn't get derailed by the sudden lack of sound coming from her phone.'

'Well, if it does I suppose we can rule this one out as another false alarm. You'd have to be a new kind of stupid to be more interested in your phone than the Mac-Tonic™ formula.'

(It was true: as hopelessly addicted to her phone and that maddening game as she was, Kathleen de la Cruz's full attention was, for once, on her daughter.)

'I've had a quick look through her inbox and sent messages,' Brenda said, staring at her monitor. 'The spelling is so bad it could almost pass for code. Nothing even remotely of interest though, unless you happen to be this Dwayne character she's got the hots for. No mention of M-T™.'

'Similar story on social media,' Cameron replied, gazing at his own screen. 'Although she does appear to have switched from M-T™ to Delixir™.'

'Noted.'

They both listened to the conversation taking place a thousand miles away.

'The boy sounds like a real moron,' Cameron said.

Brenda nodded, but there was something about the girl's voice that piqued her interest. She'd eavesdropped on enough recordings of people being tortured to know when someone was telling the truth.

She turned abruptly to Cameron.

'I think we need to escalate this. Send in the black helicopters.'

'You think?' Cameron closed his eyes and listened hard. 'I'm not sure.'

Brenda chewed her gum more vigorously.

'I know it's a long shot, but do you really want to be responsible for the Mac-Tonic™ formula falling into the wrong hands? You've heard of rendition, right?'

Cameron suddenly looked unwell. Then his eyes widened.

'Oh my God,' he said. 'The boy is talking about trying to sell it online!'

'OK, down all devices at that property. Total blackout. I'm sending this upstairs.'

Brenda ripped the headphones from her head, pushed herself away from the desk and sprinted to the control centre at the back of the room.

An Act of Selfless Martyrdom

'Stupid thing,' Ma said, banging her phone against the doorjamb.

'What?' Chuckie said. He was sitting on the floor of the hall, his back to Queenie's door, with a tablet resting on his legs.

'My phone's not working.'

Chuckie rolled his eyes. 'Well, did you *charge* it?'

'Of course I charged it!' She waddled into the TV room and plugged the phone in. Nothing happened. 'It isn't working!'

Chuckie rolled his eyes again. He was like one of those porcelain dolls.

'Well, you did just whack it on the door. What do you expect?'

Ma hollered something back, but Chuckie didn't hear. His tablet screen had just gone black. Chuckie stared down at a dim reflection of his grubby face.

'What the . . .?' His head snapped up. 'Ma! *Ma!* The tablet just died.'

'Goddamn technology. Maybe there was a power surge?'

Chuckie scowled at the doorway. He sometimes wondered where he acquired his fine intellect.

'It's a tablet, Ma! It's not plugged in!'

'Well, I don't know how these things work, do I?'

She was switching the plug on and off, like a pigeon pecking a button and waiting for a treat.

'Queenie!' she yelled. 'Queenie! Get out here and fix this phone.'

Queenie didn't move. She was still leaning against her bedroom door, studying the scribbled list of ingredients. Normally the shouting matches between her family were like white noise to her, but for some reason this argument was penetrating. With one foot planted at the base of the door, she leaned over to the ancient desktop computer beside her bed and pushed the power button. It stirred and whirred into life, and the little green light above the button blinked. But then, just as it seemed to be warming up – these old machines were like planes on a runway, building noisily to take-off – it suddenly died with a clunk and a wheeze.

And that was when she heard the distant thud of helicopter blades.

It wasn't unusual to hear choppers passing overhead: the police were always out looking for a gunman; the news networks were always following a high-speed chase; some hapless surfer was for ever in need of rescue farther down the coast. But Queenie sensed there was something different about the sound now. It seemed louder, or closer, or a slightly different pitch.

She was just being paranoid. There was probably a perfectly reasonable explanation for three separate devices dying within seconds of each other.

'TV's working!' Chuckie hollered.

The helicopter blades grew louder. Queenie left her position by the door and crossed over to the window. She pulled back the thin curtain and peered out.

A black helicopter was holding its position out over the ocean. There was a slight change in the engine noise, even though the chopper hadn't moved, and Queenie suddenly became aware of another helicopter over to the right, and then another to the left. The noses of all three helicopters were pointed directly at Queenie's house.

She let the curtain fall with a stab of dread. Out in the TV room, she could hear what sounded like an action movie but was probably the news.

'Ma!' Chuckie shouted. 'Have you seen the choppers outside?'

'What?' There was a pause, filled with the shuffling scrape of flip-flops crossing the floor. 'Oh my God! What's happening? What do they want?'

Chuckie may not have been the brightest bauble on the tree, but every once in a while he was worth looking at.

'The formula!' he said. 'They must know!'

'How could they know?' Ma asked. '*We* only just found out about it.'

She was trying to sound scornful and derisive, as she often did when talking to her children, but it didn't come off. She just sounded scared.

'Maybe Queenie's been running her mouth to someone she shouldn't?'

'Oh my God,' Ma said. Then she said it again. 'Oh my God!'

'What do you think they'll do?' Chuckie asked. He sounded excited. His sister was in big trouble, after all.

'I don't know,' Ma said. 'Who are they? What can they do?'

They were two very good questions, but only a handful of people were in a position to answer them. Chuckie, alas, was not one of the chosen few.

'Go get Queenie,' Ma said.

Chuckie didn't want to move. Outside was suddenly worth looking at. It was like the window had become a TV.

'Now!' Ma said.

Chuckie reluctantly obeyed. He hammered on Queenie's door with his fist.

'Queenie! Get on out here!' He paused for a moment, but then he thought of missing the drama outside and lost his patience. 'Queenie!'

Chuckie grabbed the handle and threw his shoulder against the door. It flew open, and he went tumbling to the floor. He got up, his cheeks burning, half expecting to find his sister off to one side, doubled over with laughter. But the room was empty. Queenie was gone.

'Ma!' Chuckie called, getting to his feet and stumbling out into the hallway. He was about to holler again when he glanced along the corridor and spotted Queenie in the kitchen.

'Queenie, what the hell have you done?' he said, striding towards her. 'We're surrounded by goddamn helicopters!'

Queenie had her back to Chuckie, but she didn't turn round. Even when he was close enough to spit in her hair, or kick her in the back of the knee, or just plain box her up the back of her head, she didn't turn round. It made Chuckie curious. He stopped yelling.

'What are you doing?' he asked.

She was standing at the cooker, and he peered around her shoulder just in time to see the Mac-Tonic™ formula catch the flames. It didn't burn like a piece of paper. Instead it curled up on itself, transforming into a wet-looking blob of plastic that Queenie dropped on to the burner.

When Queenie turned round, Chuckie's mouth was hanging open.

'You burnt it,' he whispered. Chuckie never whispered; he was clearly in shock. But then the magnitude of what his sister had done hit home, and he began to shout.

'Ma! Come quick! Queenie burnt up the recipe!'

There was real hatred in his eyes, and saliva strung itself between his teeth every time he opened his mouth to yell. Queenie heard her mother's heavy footsteps moving through the house, and fear began to unfurl itself in her stomach, but she stood firm with her back to the cooker and her hands balled into fists.

A thin, tickly smell of melted plastic hung in the air, and it seemed to be this that stopped Ma in the doorway – this which confirmed her good-for-nothing daughter had actually drilled into a whole new stratum of stupid, previously untapped by the de la Cruz line.

'What have you done, you foolish girl? Do you have any idea how much that recipe must be worth?' Her eyes bulged from her podgy face, and her massive frame seemed to quiver with rage. She was like a static hurricane. 'We could have moved to a nicer place, and got one of those double-door refrigerators and a pool and an SUV! We could have had it all, and instead we're stuck here in this dump! And it's all because of you! That damn scrap of paper was worth millions to us!'

'Billions!' Chuckie yelled.

'Trillions,' Queenie said, quietly.

The de la Cruz family stood in silence – the only sound was the reverberating thrum of the helicopters and the sickly swash of the ocean.

'What did you say?' Ma asked. Her voice wasn't raised any more, but she could barely keep the rage from boiling over. This, Queenie knew, was the eye of the storm. She tried to keep the fear from her voice, but it shook all the same.

'It's worth trillions of dollars. Not millions or billions. Trillions.'

'You trying to play smart with me?' Ma asked, stepping forwards. 'How does that make the situation any better?'

Ma was almost upon her, and Queenie was frightened. Once, back in Kansas, she'd seen Ma hit Pa around the back of the head with a steel chair for blowing twenty dollars on lottery tickets. God only knew what the penalty for losing a trillion-dollar recipe was.

'I just think you should know how much it's worth,' Queenie said. 'Before they come knocking.'

Ma stopped. The fury rolled off her like heat. She opened her mouth to speak but didn't get the chance.

There was a knock at the door.

Chuckie looked at Ma. Ma looked at Chuckie. They both looked at Queenie. Neither of them moved.

'Well,' Queenie said, stepping between them. 'I guess somebody's got to answer that.'

She walked towards the front door on trembling legs, like someone who had somehow survived a twenty-car pile-up, only to find herself walking across four lanes of traffic. In the kitchen, whoever was on the other side of the front door had seemed like a saviour. Nothing could be worse than her rampaging mother. But now, as she drew nearer, it seemed as though the front door would open on to something monstrous, something so terrifying that it would make her turn and run into Ma's arms.

She paused with her hand on the doorknob, and suddenly realized that she couldn't hear the helicopters any more. Queenie couldn't help but conclude that whatever waited on the other side of the door had been the reason for their departure. It suggested a power greater than she could imagine.

Queenie twisted the handle and opened the door.

On the porch outside, like three bears from a fairy tale, stood three men wearing immaculate grey suits with Mac-Tonic™ badges pinned to their lapels. They smiled warmly, and the man in the middle held out his hand.

'Good afternoon,' he said. There was a Southern twang to his voice that was seldom heard in North Nitch. Queenie reached out and tentatively shook his hand. It was a firm handshake, a real deal-sealer.

'It's a pleasure to meet you, Miss de la Cruz. My name is Randy van de Velde, and these are my colleagues: Alexander Greenberg and Martin DeWitt. We are here on behalf of The Mac-Tonic™ Corporation. May we step inside for a few moments?'

Queenie glanced over her shoulder. At the end of the hall, Chuckie and Ma peered around the kitchen door. She turned back to the Mac-Tonic™ trio.

'Good afternoon, Mrs de la Cruz,' Randy van de Velde said, leaning slightly to one side to get a better look down the hall. 'It's a fine place you have here. I was just speaking to your daughter about borrowing a few moments of your time.' He paused for three seconds. He seemed to be counting them out in his head. 'We have a proposal that y'all might want to consider.'

Ma came bustling along the corridor with Chuckie in tow, beckoning the three men inside. 'Of course, of course,' she said. 'Why don't you step aside, Queenie, and let these gentlemen in?'

Queenie stepped aside and let the gentlemen in. Randy van de Velde and Martin DeWitt followed Ma and Chuckie to the TV room, but Alexander Greenberg stopped at the threshold and waited for Queenie to go ahead. When she was safely inside, he closed the front door softly behind him.

'Please take a seat,' Ma said, indicating the sagging couch. It looked like a chunk of soft cheese that had been left out at room temperature for too long. The three men squeezed on to it and clasped their hands on their knees.

'Can I fetch you a drink?' Ma asked.

'We wouldn't like to put you to any trouble,' Randy van de Velde said.

'It's no trouble,' Ma said, smiling, and off she went. She was suddenly as gay as a schoolgirl.

Chuckie sat on an armchair to one side of the room, staring hard at the three men on the couch, but they only had eyes for Queenie. She stood close to the window, trying to pretend that she wasn't the subject of such scrutiny.

Ma came back with a plastic tray and set it down on the small table in front of the couch. The three men looked at the refreshments, and then they looked at Ma. She had done something unthinkable: she had served them Delixir™.

'Thank you, ma'am,' said Randy van de Velde, glossing over her faux pas. He exchanged a meaningful

look with Alexander Greenberg and Martin DeWitt –
the kind of look that prepared them for an act of selfless
martyrdom – snatched up the middle can and pressed
it to his lips.

In the years to come, the exact amount of Delixir™
that Randy van de Velde consumed that day would
become a hotly contested point of Mac-Tonic™ lore. Did
he drink too much, or not enough? Was it the right thing
to do? Should he be celebrated, or should he be
condemned? These were big questions. In some
retellings, he drained the whole can, flipped it upside
down and slammed it back on to the tray. In other
versions, he took a tiny sip that almost killed him. Either
account could be true – they were both so alluring.
When the Marketing department found out about the
episode, they made sure that many versions were kept
alive. They took cuttings from the truth and planted
them in the rich soil of rumour and whispered
encouragement to them each morning. The new shoots
thrived and blossomed and cross-pollinated with each
other. The truths are a beautiful thing.

But this was all in the future.

In the moment itself, neither Alexander Greenberg
nor Martin DeWitt were prepared for Randy van de

Velde's recklessness – even with the meaningful glance – but they hid their repulsion and awe well.

Randy van de Velde wiped his lips with the back of his hand. The repercussions would have to wait.

'I notice from your accent that you're not originally from these parts,' he said, addressing Ma but looking at Queenie.

'We hail from Kansas.'

'Ah,' Randy said. 'I had a great-aunt who lived in Kansas. It's a beautiful place.'

Queenie and Chuckie wondered whether Randy van de Velde had ever been to Kansas. They'd never heard anybody describe it as beautiful before. Maybe it became beautiful at a height of 40,000 feet.

'It's pretty flat,' Ma said, but it wasn't clear whether she was agreeing or disagreeing with Randy van de Velde.

Chuckie was bored already. Real life really sucked compared to TV.

'What are you doing here?' he asked. 'How'd you know where to find us?'

The three men turned to look at Chuckie.

'If you came for the recipe, you're too late. Queenie burnt it.'

'Shhh, Chuckie,' Ma said.

'What? It's true.'

The three men on the couch lost their air of affability at once.

'Is it true?' Alexander Greenberg asked.

All eyes turned to Queenie. She shrugged casually, although her heart threatened to beat a path right out of its cage.

'Yeah, I burnt it up.'

Randy van de Velde lost his composure. 'Why would you do a thing like that? *Why?*'

Queenie shrugged again. 'I didn't think it was the kind of thing to be left lying around. I thought you of all people would be able to see that.'

Randy van de Velde seriously thought he might have a heart attack. Recovering the recipe was supposed to be his way back into the fold, his shortcut to the top. To hear that some girl had incinerated his golden ticket was almost too much to bear. He wondered whether his luck would ever change.

And then it did.

'How much are you willing to pay for it?' Queenie asked.

Everyone was confused.

'Excuse me?' Randy van de Velde said.

'I asked you how much you'd be willing to pay for the recipe.'

Randy van de Velde didn't reply for a long time. He narrowed his eyes.

'What are you saying, little girl?'

Queenie raised her eyebrows and folded her arms. Randy van de Velde was trying to intimidate her, but it only made her more determined to get the best of him.

'Well, obviously I memorized the formula before I destroyed it.'

Randy van de Velde's face broke into a smile.

'All right,' he said, sitting forwards. 'Now we're getting somewhere. So this is a negotiation?'

'That's right,' Queenie said. 'And if the price is right, I'll tell you how to make your precious soda.'

Randy van de Velde couldn't believe his luck. He was the best goddamn salesman Mac-Tonic™ ever saw, and this hick girl wanted to go up against him in the deal? This was like Scrappy-Doo picking a fight with Muhammad Ali.

'Let's just say, if you share the formula with us, your momma will never have to work again, and neither will you or your brother, and neither will your kids.'

'I want a number,' Queenie said.

Randy van de Velde reached into his jacket pocket and took out a chequebook.

'How does a million dollars sound?'

Queenie snorted. 'Sounds like you're trying to rip us off.'

'OK,' Randy van de Velde said, smiling the situation away. 'I hear you. How about two million dollars?' Queenie opened her mouth but Randy van de Velde beat her to it. 'Tell you what, let's call it three? One million for each of you.'

Queenie didn't say anything. Ma stared at her as though, for the very first time, she was beginning to understand why people have children. *This* was the magic of motherhood.

Queenie remained silent. *Three million dollars . . .*

This is a lot like fishing, Randy van de Velde thought. *You just gotta bide your time.*

'Why isn't Dwight Eagleman here?' Queenie asked.

Randy van de Velde snapped out of his reverie. He had been imagining himself on the bank of a tranquil stream, waiting for the trout to bite.

'Mr Eagleman is a very busy man, and I'm sure if he could be here, he would be.'

Queenie considered this.

'I think if Mr Eagleman was here, he'd be offering me a lot more than three million dollars.'

'Yeah,' Chuckie said. 'If you want the recipe so much, why isn't that guy from the TV here?'

'Look,' said Alexander Greenberg. 'Our offer is generous – very generous. We appreciate your help in locating the formula, but it might be worth remembering that the formula belongs to The Mac-Tonic™ Corporation. What we're offering here is in recognition of your efforts. You do not own the formula; it is not yours to sell.'

'Think about what you could do with three million dollars, Mrs de la Cruz,' Martin DeWitt said, smiling warmly. 'This place here is swell, but you could move to an even nicer place with a pool, maybe treat yourself to one of those double-door refrigerators. Drive a shiny, new SUV straight off the showroom floor. Just think about what's on the table here.'

'And this deal won't be on the table for ever,' Alexander Greenberg said. 'And when it's gone, it'll be gone for good. We're close to reverse-engineering the formula, you know?'

Alexander Greenberg and Martin DeWitt turned to look at Randy van de Velde. He was unusually quiet. This was because he was thinking really hard – something he didn't like to do too often. Queenie was beginning to squirm under his silent gaze. In fact, she was beginning to squirm anyway: the effects of the Mac-Tonic™ were beginning to wear off. She felt suddenly weak and clammy. She leaned back against the wall to make sure she didn't sway.

Randy van de Velde had noticed this. He knew the signs well enough. Queenie may have been making things difficult, but she *wanted* him to have the formula. The sooner she had access to a supply of Mac-Tonic™, the better.

'Queenie,' Randy van de Velde said. 'How about, in addition to the money, we throw in a lifetime supply of Mac-Tonic™, as a personal thank you?'

Queenie didn't feel like she could make a decision. The wall felt hot against her back.

'You'd never have to buy another bottle,' Randy van de Velde said. 'You could drink a gallon a day, if it suited you.'

'Just tell him the formula,' Ma said. Then she turned to Randy van de Velde and said, 'Write the cheque. Make it out to me.'

Randy van de Velde withdrew a pen from his jacket pocket and held it above the chequebook. He smiled at Queenie. It made her feel queasy. She had to get out.

'I'll be right back,' she said.

She dashed from the room, out the front door, and scrambled under the house. Her mouth started salivating the moment she saw the two cans of Mac-Tonic™. She downed the first one in a succession of painful gulps. She belched and was almost sick. She snapped open the second can and took a more discerning sip. The shakes began to steady, the dizziness evened out. She took another sip. She began to feel normal again. She crawled out from beneath the house.

She resolved to accept Randy van de Velde's offer. She didn't care if three million dollars was a steal: it was more money than she could ever hope to have, and all she'd had to do for it was pick up a piece of trash.

She turned towards the house, put a foot on the bottom step, and a black bag was yanked over her head. Strong arms dragged her backwards and threw her down on to a hard surface. An engine revved, and she slid on her side into something that echoed with a hollow, metallic thud.

Randy van de Velde, Alexander Greenberg and Martin DeWitt burst out on to the porch.

Queenie de la Cruz was gone.

A can of Mac-Tonic™ glugged itself empty on to the sand.

Communist Aliens

'It's day fourteen of the Great Thirst – a whole two weeks since the last drop of Mac-Tonic™ disappeared from the shelves – and the Death-o-Meter is up at a whopping 1,337.' The newsreader paused and lifted a finger to his ear. 'And reports are just coming in from New York City, where a desperate attempt to secure the last known bottle of Mac-Tonic™ is currently underway. We can now go live to the scene, where Samantha has more.'

Samantha's face appeared onscreen beside the newsreader's: she had blonde hair, white teeth and a microphone held just beneath her chin. Her expression was a practised combination of polite concern and rabid excitement. The Statue of Liberty loomed up behind her, giant and green and bored out of her mind.

'Thanks, Bruce. I'm here on Liberty Island where someone has taken matters into their own hands. Or should that be . . . Lady Liberty's hands?'

The camera panned up the Statue of Liberty and zoomed in on the hand that held a huge bottle of Mac-Tonic™ aloft. Halfway up the forearm, clinging on for dear life, was a man intent on reaching the tantalizing prize.

'Eyewitnesses claim that the man – as yet unidentified – climbed out of one of the windows in Lady Liberty's crown to begin his daredevil ascent. He has no harness or safety net, so if he slips it'll be a 300-foot fall to the ground below.'

Samantha's expression was solemn, but you could tell she was delighted to have another potential casualty to add to the Death-o-Meter. The eyes gave it away. In the bottom corner of the screen, the digits of the Death-o-Meter ticked over until they reached 1,340. The graphic flashed like a one-armed bandit hitting the jackpot.

'High stakes indeed,' Bruce said, his smile glossing over all matters of delicacy and taste. 'Can you tell us what's actually in that bottle?'

There was a brief pause while a network of satellites relayed the question to Samantha. She smiled like a contestant on a game show. In the background, the man clung on like a baby monkey.

'Well, Bruce, that's the real tragedy here. The Mac-Tonic™ Corporation dismissed rumours that the bottle was full of their delicious, thirst-quenching soda long ago, so even if that man does reach the summit, it will all be for nothing.'

'That's too bad, Sam. That's just too bad.' Samantha's feed was cut, and Bruce once again had the whole screen to himself. 'We'll keep you updated on that story as it develops, folks.

'Meanwhile, in related news, reclusive Delixir™ CEO Teddy Ritzendollar reported a two point five per cent uplift in sales last month. Ritzendollar has been issuing statements from an undisclosed location ever since the Great Thirst began, following a barrage of death threats from disgruntled Mac-Tonic™ consumers.'

Bruce once again lifted a hand to his ear. He looked away from the camera and rested a hand on the desk. In the corner of the screen, the Death-o-Meter rolled over to 1,341.

Bruce suddenly sat up straight. He stared down the barrel of the camera. His expression switched from friendly confidant to concerned father. There was every indication that the next words he uttered might well be the most important of his career, and the viewer's life.

'Breaking news.' He actually said those words. 'The Mac-Tonic™ formula has been found. I'll say that again: the Mac-Tonic™ formula has been found. We can now go live to Stacey in North Nitch, California.'

Another reporter's face filled the screen. It was one of the mysteries of the modern world how news networks always managed to have someone on the scene seconds after an incident. They had a better response rate than the emergency services. Any faster, and they'd be suspects in the cases they covered.

'Thanks, Bruce. The town of North Nitch isn't known for much around these parts, but from this day on it will always be famed as the place where the Mac-Tonic™ recipe was rediscovered. According to an official Mac-Tonic™ press release, the formula *washed up* on the shoreline here, where it was found by a girl, identified by locals as' – Stacey checked a cue card – 'Queenie de la Cruz.'

Bruce looked like he'd found the recipe all by himself. 'This news will come as a huge relief to the millions of people who have gone two weeks without so much as a drop of Mac-Tonic™. Has the company revealed a timeline for when the drink might be back on the shelves?'

Stacey's smile faltered slightly.

'Well, Bruce, this is where things get *really* interesting. Shortly after Miss de la Cruz found the recipe, high-ranking representatives from The Mac-Tonic™ Corporation arranged to collect it *in person* from the house behind me. By the time they arrived, Miss de la Cruz had been abducted.'

Bruce looked crushed. He was pretty strung out on cheap store soda, and the prospect of going without Mac-Tonic™ indefinitely, when an end had seemed so close, was almost too much to bear.

'Who's behind this?' he demanded.

'Well,' Stacey said, 'there is currently very little evidence for the authorities to go on. All we know so far is that the kidnappers took off in a black van with Nevada plates, but the identity of the abductors – and their motives – remain a mystery.

'This turn of events also raises the tantalizing prospect that the two missing Mac-Tonic™ executives are still alive out there somewhere, although with each passing day their chances of survival grow slimmer and slimmer.'

'Thanks, Stacey.'

Stacey disappeared from the screen. The Death-o-Meter reached 1,350. The designers of the graphic had programmed it to spout a little shower of confetti every time the number hit a milestone of fifty or one hundred, accompanied by a tinkling sound.

'Well,' Bruce said, regaining some of his composure, 'this is really the most remarkable turn of events. We're joined now by Dr Dick Wannamaker, an authority on speculative theories, as well as Desmond Clutterbuck, who specializes in air crash investigations . . .'

What followed was a heated and largely pointless debate between two people with some pretty far-fetched ideas. The upshot was that by the end of the segment, Queenie had been incorrectly labelled as a Mexican immigrant, and the circumstances surrounding her disappearance had been distorted into a grotesque work of paranoid fantasy. By the time the debate was concluded, the banner across the bottom of the screen read:

MAC-TONIC™ EXECS TURN TO CANNIBALISM
AFTER COMMUNIST ALIENS CRASH PLANE AND
ABDUCT MEXICAN GIRL FOR FORMULA

Just before the network cut to a commercial break, Bruce Dillinger pressed a finger to his earpiece one final time.

'This just in: The Mac-Tonic™ Corporation is offering a ten-million-dollar reward to anyone who provides information leading to the safe recovery of the recipe.'

Earl McLaughlin stopped cleaning his rifle and glanced up at the TV screen. A bead of sweat rolled across his scarred scalp and dripped on to his vest. He set the rifle down at the end of a row of firearms on the rough wooden floor.

'Cody,' he called.

Slow, heavy footsteps resonated through the boards. A muscular man in jeans, boots and nothing else appeared in the doorway. He lifted a hand to his mouth and removed the damp cigarette butt that was clamped there. His fingers were dark with grease and oil.

'What?' he asked.

Earl jutted his chin at the TV screen. The implausible news headline was still scrolling along the bottom. Cody did not seem to find it alarming.

'Get the truck ready,' Earl said. 'We're goin' to Nevada.'

A Desperate Attempt to Save Human Civilization

'What the hell were they thinking?' Dwight Eagleman said. He was standing behind his chair, his hands gripping the headrest like a pair of claws. The men around the table were meek under his piercing stare. The Kennedy Kid couldn't help but gawp: he'd never seen his father so angry. 'I mean, who in their right mind writes down the world's most valuable secret, puts it in a bottle and sends it out to be discovered by a complete stranger?'

There were mumbles of agreement. It was a darn stupid thing to do. Randy van de Velde cleared his throat, and suddenly all eyes were on him.

'I don't think they were in their right minds, Dwight.' He looked apologetic. 'I heard they ate each other.'

Dwight Eagleman just stared. If looks could kill, Randy van de Velde would have been seriously regretting not picking out a headstone and epitaph for himself before now. No doubt Marcie would choose something tacky and maudlin and he'd be turning in his grave every time he thought about it. He made a mental note to visit a funeral director at the next available opportunity.

Dwight Eagleman was still staring.

'And where did you hear that piece of information, Randy?'

'It was on TV.'

'It was on TV.' Dwight Eagleman's voice was flat, dreamlike, scornful. He rarely mocked people directly: it was not a great way of winning them over, and people were much easier to manipulate if they liked you. He preferred a more covert approach, but to hell with it: he didn't need Randy van de Velde to like him. 'And how would some TV station hack come to know a thing like that?'

Randy van de Velde looked decidedly uncomfortable.

'He was an expert.'

'Goddamnit, Randy! Stop getting your information from the damn television!'

Dwight Eagleman turned away from the table and put his hands on his hips. Beyond the glass, the skyscrapers of Manhattan jostled around the Mac-Tonic™ building like penguins that knew the world was a frigid, unforgiving place outside the huddle. The company's share price had spiked the moment the news about the message in a bottle broke, but Queenie's abduction had sent it crashing down again, and The Mac-Tonic™ Corporation was beginning to look cursed. Diseased. Forsaken. Dwight Eagleman knew it would take some time for M-T™ to be cast out, but it was all about money, and money had no heart, no feelings, no memory. He'd have to time the resurrection perfectly. The greatest company on earth was a few missteps away from extinction, and the next couple of plays would be critical. He had to get everything just right.

Dwight Eagleman allowed himself to feel the weight of that responsibility, and knew immediately that it was a burden he could carry. He turned back to the room.

'Here is what we are going to do. Alexander, I would like you to give a press conference. It's vital that we get a handle on this situation – that the people think we are in control. We need to really push that reward money. Take a suitcase full of cash to the press conference if you have to. Let the people see the dollars, and remind them of what finding the recipe means: it means restoring an American institution; it means becoming a national hero; it means reviving the soft drink that their fondest memories are steeped in.'

Alexander Greenberg nodded. 'It might be worth pursuing the human interest element? Say something about this little girl. What's her name again?'

'De la Cruz,' Martin DeWitt said, checking a memo. 'Queenie de la Cruz.'

'She's Mexican, I think,' Randy van de Velde said helpfully.

'She's not Mexican,' said Silvio Rizzuto. 'She's from Kansas.'

'But . . .' Randy van de Velde said. 'Her name . . .'

Randy van de Velde's mind was imploding. It was like someone was trying to upload twenty-first century software on to a computer from the late 70s.

'She is descended from a Spaniard who fled religious persecution in the eighteenth century,' said Silvio Rizzuto. 'That's where her name comes from. I've got a whole file on her here.'

Randy van de Velde sulked in his seat. He just could not catch a break these days.

'Gentlemen,' said Dwight Eagleman, 'Alexander is right. We need to stop thinking of Queenie de la Cruz as a little girl, and start thinking of her as a trillion-dollar asset. We need to make her central to our appeal. Make it seem like we want to find *her*, instead of the recipe. Get her family on morning TV and all the late shows. A crying mother is campaign gold dust. Use it.'

'What about the people on the planes?' the Kennedy Kid asked. 'Mr Funderburk and Mr Hewitt? The pilots and air hostesses?'

'What about them?'

'Well, they might still be alive out there.'

Dwight Eagleman sighed and stared hard at his son.

'Alexander, make sure you renew our pledge to find Lyle and Lewie at the press conference. Promise that no expense will be spared in rescuing them. Paint them as heroes. Their message in a bottle was a desperate attempt to save human civilization.'

Alexander Greenberg nodded.

'And remember to mention the pilot and crew as well,' Dwight Eagleman added, as an afterthought. 'But make sure they don't sound like an afterthought.'

'I'll handle it.'

The Kennedy Kid's heart soared. After weeks of being ignored and ridiculed he'd finally contributed something that his father approved of. Finally, he began to feel part of this strange, exotic flock. It was wonderful.

Dwight Eagleman sat down in his chair. There were two bowls on the table before him: one was empty, and the other was filled with plump strawberries. He picked up the small, ivory-handled knife resting between them.

'Do we know who was behind the abduction?' he asked.

Alexander Greenberg, Martin DeWitt and Randy van de Velde looked sheepish. The abduction had happened on their watch, after all. The formula had been in their grasp and they'd let it slip away. Randy van de Velde looked particularly shamefaced. If it transpired that he'd drunk Delixir™ for nothing, he was pretty sure he'd have to change his name and move to Siberia.

'No,' said Alexander Greenberg. 'But I think we all know who the prime suspect is.'

The executives exchanged meaningful glances. It was company policy not to mention Delixir™ by name unless absolutely necessary. Dwight Eagleman picked up a strawberry and placed the blade against its flesh.

'And what are the latest figures from our competitor?'

Martin DeWitt shuffled the papers before him, even though he knew exactly what the latest figures were.

'Sales volume for the competition is up two point five per cent.'

With a twitch of his fingers, Dwight Eagleman scalped the strawberry. Its crown fell into the empty bowl.

'That will be all,' he said.

The board got to their feet and headed towards the door. Dwight Eagleman picked up another strawberry and held it so that the knife was partially embedded in the fruit. He sensed someone lingering on the far side of the table. He did not look up.

'What is it?'

The Kennedy Kid cleared his throat.

'I was just wondering how many extra planes you're going to send to search for Mr Funderburk, Mr Hewitt and the others?'

Dwight Eagleman sliced the top off the strawberry and picked up another.

'None,' he said.

Another flick of the wrist, another crown in the bowl.

'How many are currently searching for them?'

Dwight Eagleman looked up and smiled placidly. He picked up another strawberry.

'Currently? None.'

The Kennedy Kid opened to his mouth to speak but stuttered, and hated himself for it.

'S-So you're *not* going to look for them? But you just said—'

'I know what I said.'

Dwight Eagleman's attention was back on the ivory-handled knife.

'But . . .' The Kennedy Kid was at a loss. 'I mean, they could still be alive out there, Dad.'

The CEO of The Mac-Tonic™ Corporation looked up and held the Kennedy Kid's wounded gaze.

'I hope they are, son. I really hope they are. Do you have any idea how reckless their actions were? How their selfishness could have destroyed this company?'

He paused. He was still holding a strawberry beneath the blade. When he spoke, his words were heavy with menace.

'Throughout this company's history, many people have threatened its prosperity, and in each case they have been removed without hesitation, without ceremony and without regret. Even Horatio Macfarlane, the founder of this great company, was silenced by his own creation when he began to lose his grip. So do not pity those two men: they would not want to be rescued. Not now. In the eyes of The Mac-Tonic™ Corporation, they are beyond redemption.'

The Kennedy Kid's eyes filled with hot, stinging tears, but he didn't wipe them away. His father – the man he'd always looked up to, the man he'd been desperate to impress, the man he thought he'd wanted to become – was dissolving in his tears. But he refused to blink.

'And in my eyes,' the Kennedy Kid said, 'so are you.'

He turned away from his father and slipped out through the frosted glass door. Dwight Eagleman watched the dark silhouette of his son fade to nothing. Then he looked down at the strawberry between his fingers.

A moment later, the blade slipped through its flesh, and its crown dropped into the waiting bowl.

A Strong Lead

The black van with Nevada plates hurtled through the desert. There was hardly any traffic on the road; it passed more billboards than cars. They were visible from miles away, looming large as the van approached and passed beneath them like a tugboat in the shadow of mighty ships. They were spaced at two-mile intervals, and every single one was advertising Delixir™.

Feeling betrayed by Mac-Tonic™?
Get revenge, and serve it cold.
Drink Delixir™

Another two miles of scrubby desert rolled by. Wet mirages shimmered on the distant horizon and evaporated.

Delixir™
Quenching the desert.

Occasionally the van would pass a car at the side of the road. Most of them had obviously been abandoned for some time: they were orange with rust, and anything salvageable had been amputated long ago. But one was clearly a recent casualty: its driver tried to flag the van down. The van sped past.

Queenie was sweating profusely in the back of the van. Her captors had tied her up shortly after reaching the highway, and the rough rope cut into her wrists and ankles.

Don't panic, she told herself. *Just breathe.*

But breathing was difficult, and the trouble with telling yourself not to panic is that it reminds you just how panicky you feel. Her body was telling her to fight, or run, but she couldn't do either, and the unspent adrenaline was beginning to sap the strength from her limbs. She felt like a blancmange, and the vibrations of the engine only made the feeling worse. Queenie rested her hooded head against the floor, and tried not to think about her destination.

Don't panic. Just breathe.

Outside, the colossal Delixir™ billboards kept springing up every couple of miles, and the two men up front couldn't help but glance at them as they came into view.

> *Delicious, delightful, delectable.*
> *Delixir™*

They were getting pretty thirsty, but they were under strict instructions not to stop, and so they kept going.

Queenie had given up screaming for help a few miles on to the highway. She'd noticed that the van had stopped cornering, which meant it must be out of the residential and business districts and on to one of those endless, godforsaken highways her family had traversed to reach California. She knew, from that awful journey, what a desolate, empty place the United States of America could be. It was the kind of country – and Nevada was the kind of state – where you could safely test an atomic bomb without putting in a courtesy call to the neighbours beforehand.

She knew that screaming was pointless. She was saving her lungs for the moment they came off the highway. Then she'd let the whole damn town know where she was.

It was late in the evening when the smooth concrete of the highway gave way to a bumpy, rutted track, and the van began snaking from side to side. Queenie could hear the roar of gravel beneath the tyres, and with every jolt a rib or hip or shoulder would grind against the textured metal flooring. Her whole body was in a state of extreme cramp from being bound for so long.

When the van finally slowed to a stop, she was about ready to claw someone's eyes out.

'You goddamn pigs! Let me out of here!' She struggled against the rope around her wrists and ankles. The cloth of the hood filled her mouth as she sucked a breath into her constricted lungs. She spat it out. 'I'll kill you all, you hear me!'

There was a voice from outside, and it gave her hope.

'Hey!' she screamed. 'Hey! Help me!'

There was laughter, and her moment of hope vanished.

'Sounds like you've got a live one in there,' the voice said.

'Well,' said someone in the van, as though this was an exchange he'd had a hundred times before, 'she wouldn't be much use to us dead.'

The man outside laughed. Queenie's blood ran cold.

'Well, don't let me keep you. Go on in.'

There was a crunch of small stones as the van pulled away. Queenie breathed into the wet fabric of the hood and clenched her teeth.

The van trundled along the track for another couple of miles and then came to a stop. The driver killed the engine.

'Man, I hate that drive,' he said.

A second later the side door rolled open. Feet shuffled close to Queenie's head and she was lifted clean off the floor. A strong pair of hands held each of her limbs.

'Let me go, you morons! Put me down!'

'Trust us, young lady, you wouldn't want us to put you down here if you could see where we are.'

There was an edge to the man's voice that made Queenie's breath catch in her throat. Or maybe it was all the contortion and suspension. Either way, she fell silent and listened.

At first, she couldn't hear anything beyond the men's breathing and the scuffing of their boots as they stepped down from the van. There was no surf. No traffic. No whispering crops. No lowing cattle. Nothing. Just a heat that was almost audible. She thought she heard an insect, a lonely cicada calling for a mate, but she couldn't be sure. A hot breeze ripped at her T-shirt and rattled something brittle nearby.

Queenie was struck by the sickening realization that if she screamed, no one would hear her.

A door groaned open. It sounded heavy. A second later the stifling heat was replaced by a delicious coolness. The door groaned shut. It was even quieter inside than it had been outside. Queenie was carried between the men like a particularly heavy picnic hamper. Their footsteps bounced off the walls and made the place sound both empty and busy at the same time. She couldn't tell when they turned a corner because of the constant to-ing and fro-ing between the men.

Finally, another door opened with a squeal, followed quickly by another, and Queenie was thrown on the floor. The ropes around her ankles and wrists were untied, and Queenie whimpered as her muscles relaxed. Fresh bouts of excruciating cramp gnawed at her hamstrings and calves. Little pieces of grit dug into her cheek through the damp hood. But Queenie didn't move.

The footsteps receded, the door squealed shut and a heavy key was turned in the lock.

Queenie lay still, breathing deeply. The cramp worsened, and she groaned through her teeth.

'Are you OK?' someone asked.

Queenie hadn't been moving before, but now she could have passed for a corpse. She stopped groaning and held her breath.

'Who's there?' she asked.

'It's all right,' the voice said.

She couldn't tell if it was a man's voice or a boy's, but the sound of approaching footsteps made her scramble to remove the hood from her head. Her arms felt like someone else's – or like someone had amputated her arms and was still trying to use them – but eventually she yanked it off. The room was dim, but what little light there was made her squint. She tried to get up but found that her legs wouldn't respond. She fell back and scurried away until her back bumped against a wall.

She shielded her eyes, and the outline of a person took shape. He had stopped moving the moment Queenie began her retreat. He had his hands raised, palms facing out.

'It's OK,' he said.

'Who are you?' Queenie asked.

'My name is Todd,' he said. 'What's yours?'

'Where am I?' Queenie demanded. 'What's going on?'

Now that she was sitting up, Queenie became aware of a dull pounding in her head. She tried to recall the last time she'd had something to drink, and soon realized it was the can of Mac-Tonic™, back at home, several hours earlier.

She focused on the boy – Todd – who was definitely not a man yet. He was tall, but in a lanky, disproportionate kind of way. His shoulders were narrow and sloping, and his face was boyish and smooth. His hands were still raised, as though he was scared of what Queenie might do next.

'I don't know where we are,' Todd said. 'I can only tell you what happens here.'

Queenie blinked hard and tried to clear the ache behind her eyes. The room came into focus, and she saw what 'here' actually looked like. It was large – much too large to be a prison cell – and the walls were made of smooth, grey concrete. At the very top of the far wall, just beneath the ceiling, a narrow window stretched along the length of the room, letting in the last of the daylight. There were no light fixtures: when the sun set, the room would go dark. There was no furniture, only a plastic bucket in one corner and a faucet poking from the wall nearby, with a grille in the floor beneath.

Todd saw Queenie looking over at the bucket and lowered his head.

'If I'd have known you were coming I would have emptied the toilet.'

Queenie frowned. 'That bucket is your toilet?'

Todd nodded, finally lowering his hands. 'Our toilet.'

Queenie looked horrified. She couldn't believe she'd ended up somewhere worse than North Nitch. What were the chances?

'How long have you been here?' she asked.

Todd scratched his head and glanced at the long, narrow window.

'I think this is day thirteen,' he said. Then he seemed to doubt himself and began counting on his fingers. 'Or day fourteen.'

'You've been inside this room for *two weeks*?'

'I've been here for two weeks – wherever *here* is – but sometimes I get taken to a different room.' His face fell. 'I prefer this room, though.'

Queenie wondered what the other room must be like for this one to be preferable, but she couldn't bring herself to ask. The pounding in her head was relentless.

'What's your name again?' she asked.

Todd seemed to brighten. 'Todd.'

'OK,' she said. 'I'm Queenie.'

'Nice to meet you.'

Queenie rolled her eyes. The pain behind them flared up.

'Does that faucet over there work?'

Todd nodded.

'Good.'

Queenie got to her feet and was immediately floored by cramp. She sucked air through her teeth and dug her nails into her palms. Todd came forwards and crouched beside her.

'You've got to stretch it out,' he said. 'It'll hurt more to begin with, but then it'll get better.'

Queenie glared at him.

'Trust me,' he said. 'I was exactly the same when I got here.'

Queenie was willing to try just about anything to escape the pain, so she followed Todd's advice. He was right: at first, it felt like her tendons might snap, but then the cramping began to ease.

'It'll help if you drink some water, too,' Todd said.

He offered Queenie a hand but she slapped it away. She hauled herself up and staggered across the vast room. Todd scurried ahead and collected the bucket. Queenie opened the faucet, bent her mouth to the stream of water and slurped thirstily.

Water had never tasted so good. It was almost, in that moment, more refreshing than an ice-cold glass of Mac-Tonic™. Almost.

Queenie drank until her stomach felt bloated. Then she closed the faucet, wiped her mouth and belched. She straightened up and, after a moment of dizziness, began to feel much better. There was still the gnawing, crazing itch for *Mac-Tonic™*, but that craving had become just another of her body's unconscious, automatic functions.

She turned around to find Todd standing several paces away, holding the bucket.

'Do you mind . . .' he said, glancing meaningfully at the grille beneath the faucet.

Queenie walked over to the door while Todd poured the contents of his bucket down the drain. She studied the door: it was a slab of iron. Rounded rivets marked its perimeter. There was no window, and she could tell from the hinges that it must have been several inches thick. It was the kind of door you'd hide behind if someone told you the Incredible Hulk was coming.

She turned back to Todd, who had washed his hands and was wiping them on his jeans.

'So. Todd.' Queenie looked around the empty room. 'What do you do around here for fun?'

Todd swallowed hard and glanced nervously at the door behind her.

'It was a joke,' Queenie said. Todd smiled weakly. 'But seriously, what are you doing here?'

Todd shook his head in irritation.

'It's stupid. All I did was tell my friends that I'd worked out the Mac-Tonic™ formula, and the next day I got grabbed on my way home from school and bundled into a van. And now I'm here!'

Queenie was confused, and an uncomfortable feeling of dread was beginning to expand in her chest.

'What makes you think you're here because of that?' she asked.

Todd glanced at the door again.

'Because it's all they talk about . . . out there.'

'In the other room?'

He nodded. Queenie's back began to crawl, and she turned so that she could at least keep one eye on the door.

'What happens in there?'

Todd breathed heavily through his nose. He tried to meet Queenie's eye but couldn't.

'Torture.'

'What?'

Queenie looked at Todd. He didn't appear to have any bruises or burns or wounds, but then again, she could only see the skin of his arms, hands, face and neck. Whenever she hit Chuckie, she always made sure to do it somewhere discreet. Todd seemed to sense what she was thinking.

'It's mostly been psychological, so far. Sleep deprivation, white noise, water torture – that kind of thing. I think I'm getting off lighter than some of the others.'

'What others?'

Todd looked confused. 'We aren't the only ones being held here.'

'How do you know? Have you seen anyone else?'

'There was someone else in here, before you, but the

rest must be kept in other rooms. Sometimes you can hear them scream.'

Queenie looked at the door again, and wondered what you would have to do to someone to make their screams penetrate a door that thick.

'Besides,' Todd continued, 'if they brought me here because I joked about knowing the Mac-Tonic™ recipe, how many other people must be here for a similar reason?'

'But it doesn't make sense. Why would anyone believe those people know the formula?'

'I know,' Todd said. 'It's ridiculous. *No one* knows the formula. I think that's why they've gone fairly easy on me. I'm not one of their strong leads.'

Queenie cleared her throat. She was beginning to understand the direness of her situation. She was no Sherlock Holmes, but she supposed someone who actually knew the Mac-Tonic™ formula might be considered a strong lead. She thought again about the thickness of the door.

'Who are "they"?' she asked.

Todd's face fell.

'Isn't it obvious?' he asked. 'It has to be Mac-Tonic™ or Delixir™. Who else would be this desperate to find the formula?'

The world as Queenie saw it began to tilt. She knew it couldn't be Mac-Tonic™ – they'd been seconds away from regaining the formula when she was abducted. But could it really be Delixir™? She hated Delixir™ all right, but surely they wouldn't torture people – kids! – just to obtain their competitor's secret recipe?

Queenie had no idea how business really works.

'But . . . why?' she asked. 'What would Delixir™ even do with it?'

Todd shrugged. 'I guess they'd start making their own version.'

Queenie wondered whether Mac-Tonic™ would taste the same if it came in a Delixir™ bottle. It was an interesting thought experiment.

'Look,' Todd said, 'I didn't mean to scare you when I talked about . . . the other room. No one's come for me recently, so maybe they've found the person they need. I'm sure they'll let us go soon.'

Queenie shook her head. She was struggling to assimilate the memory of Randy van de Velde offering her three million dollars and a lifetime supply of Mac-Tonic™ with her current predicament.

'Queenie?' Todd said. 'Are you OK?'

She shook her head.

'They're going to torture me,' she mumbled. 'They're going to come for me.'

'They might not,' Todd said. 'They might have found the person they're looking for already.'

Queenie looked up. She was suddenly very alert.

'Todd, I know the recipe. I *am* the person they're looking for.'

'Oh,' said Todd.

There was a scream from somewhere beyond the door, a bloodcurdling shriek of agony. Queenie flinched.

'We have to get out of here,' Queenie said, scouring the room for a way out. She ran to the door and leaned her weight against it. Unsurprisingly, it didn't budge.

'What's beyond this door?' she asked.

'A corridor,' Todd said. He was looking at Queenie as though she were dying before his eyes. 'More rooms. It's a labyrinth.'

'And how many of them come to fetch you, when it's . . . y'know . . . time?'

'Four.'

'Could we overpower them, do you think?'

'No. They're too strong.'

'Damn!'

Queenie looked around the room. Walls. Bucket. Faucet. Window.

'What about that window?'

'We're on the fourth floor. Even if we could somehow get through it, we'd fall to our deaths.'

Queenie frowned. She couldn't remember being carried upstairs, or pausing to ascend in an elevator, but then she had been hooded, disorientated, dehydrated and in agony, so maybe she'd missed something along the way.

'What makes you think we're on the fourth floor?'

Todd shrugged. 'One of the guards mentioned it.'

Queenie looked up at the window again. The light pouring through the thin mesh was pale orange. A vague shadow passed over the right-hand pane, making Queenie flinch.

'Todd, if we're on the fourth floor, why is there a dog outside sniffing at the windows?'

Todd turned around and jumped. Sure enough, the silhouette of a skinny-looking dog was making its way along the row of windows, stopping every now and then to sniff or pee on something. Todd was confused.

'What the . . .'

'We're underground,' Queenie said, walking over to the wall and placing her hand against it. She looked up at the window directly overhead. 'That's ground level up there. Do you think if you stood on that bucket, and I climbed on your shoulders, I'd be able to reach the window?'

Todd appraised the distance. 'Maybe.'

Another chilling scream penetrated the door.

'Well, come on then!'

Todd hurried over to the bucket and flipped it upside down against the base of the wall. Queenie ran over to where her hood lay on the floor and pulled it over her right hand like an oven mitt. Todd climbed up on to the bucket and turned to face Queenie.

'Lock your hands,' she said. 'Lower, so I can step on them. Haven't you ever climbed a fence before?'

Todd shook his head. Queenie stared in disbelief. *Who is this kid?*

'Well, I suppose there's a first time for everything. Now, hold still.'

Todd did his best, but Queenie's elbows and knees dug into his shoulders and he couldn't help but squirm.

'I said, hold still!'

'I'm trying!'

Queenie got her feet on to Todd's shoulders and stood up. The plastic bucket began to bend and warp, making Todd's balance even more precarious.

'I can reach it!' Queenie called.

'Hurry up!'

Queenie slammed her covered palm against the window. The mesh reverberated, but the window held fast.

'It won't budge! I need something to break it with!'

She glanced over her shoulder and her eyes locked on to the only other thing in the room.

'I'm coming down!'

Todd caught a knee in the face before he could process what Queenie had said.

'Ow! What are you doing?'

'Hang on!'

Queenie raced across to the faucet, stood to one side and brought the sole of her shoe down on it again and again until it broke away from the wall. A stream of water gushed from the hole and pooled on the floor. Queenie grabbed the faucet, clambered up on to Todd's shoulders and began beating it against the window.

At the third blow, the window shattered. Queenie was worried that the mesh would be fastened tight to the frame, but she was able to wrench it away with a few sharp tugs. Todd wobbled dangerously beneath her, forcing her to cling to the sill.

'Are you done yet?' he asked. 'This isn't exactly comfortable.'

'Almost!'

Queenie used the faucet to knock out the shards of glass still clinging to the frame.

'All right,' she said. 'I'm going to pull myself up.'

With both hands on the frame, Queenie hauled herself through the narrow gap. Pieces of glass snagged at her clothing and scratched her skin, but it was nothing compared to what would be done to her in that other room. She rolled out on to the ground and found herself looking up at a huge expanse of sky. The first stars were beginning to shine through the dusk – or maybe they were planets or satellites or reflective bits of space junk. Queenie couldn't tell and didn't really care.

She was free.

She sat up and looked around. It was almost dark, but she could just make out a chain-link fence across an empty stretch of rough ground. Beyond the fence, the earth turned scrubby with withered plants that were either dead or dying or just plain ugly. It was a wasteland in every direction. The ground beneath her was still warm, but the air was turning chilly in the way that only desert air does. Soon it would be night-time, and then the temperature would plummet.

Queenie looked back at the building and was surprised to find a squat, single-storey monstrosity. It stretched away into the darkness, and she wondered with a shiver how big it really was, and how deep into the earth it burrowed.

'Queenie!' Todd hissed. 'Are you still there?'

Queenie got up and crouched by the window. Todd had moved away from the wall, but she could only see his outline. The cell must have been a dark and wretched place to spend the night.

'Hang on,' Queenie said. 'I'll find something to lower down to you.'

She stood up and looked about and remembered what a desolate place this was. *What the hell can I lower down? Sand? Grit? Rocks?* She ran along the length of the wall in search of something – anything – that she might be able to use. There was nothing. After a minute or so she doubled back. Panic rose in her chest, making it difficult to breathe, and she started to despair. She needed to get away from here. As she approached the broken window, she wondered whether she should just make a run for it.

Todd will be fine, she told herself. *They'll work out he doesn't know anything and let him go. It's me they want. Besides, he'll only slow me down. He's never even climbed a fence! He's probably got rich parents who are already on their way to take him home. What have I got?*

She turned towards the chain-link fence but stopped. She looked back at the small dark window she had crawled through moments earlier, and imagined being on the other side of it again, alone, looking up at a rectangle of fading light, waiting in vain for someone to return. She thought about that other room – the screams – and realized the only thing more terrifying than being tortured for something you did know was being tortured for something you didn't.

Todd's voice came again, small and uncertain. 'Queenie?'

'Oh, *hell*.' She ran back to the window and crouched down. 'Hang on!'

She ran in the opposite direction and couldn't believe her luck. Just twenty yards from the window she'd broken through was a rolled fire hose, fixed to the wall. She ran over and grabbed the still-warm nozzle. At first it wouldn't unravel. It was clearly ancient, and Queenie began to wonder whether the sun had melted the coils, fusing them together over the years. *But what kind of fire hose can't withstand heat?* She gave it a yank and the hose peeled away from itself. The reel began to turn.

When she had plenty of slack, she carried the nozzle over to the broken window and dropped it down.

'Grab on to this and I'll pull you up,' she said.

'OK,' Todd said. 'Ready.'

Queenie went back to the hose reel and began to wind it in. Todd must have been a lot heavier than he looked, because it was much harder work than Queenie had anticipated. Her arms were still tender from being bound in the van, and at one point she thought the hose would slip and send Todd plummeting back into the cell.

When the hose suddenly lost all its tension, Queenie went sprawling to the ground. By the time she had regained her feet, a dark shape was clambering out of the low window.

Todd stood up and dusted himself off.

'What now?' he asked.

Queenie looked out at the fading landscape beyond the chain-link perimeter.

'Now,' Queenie said, 'you get to climb your first fence.'

They ran over and Queenie interlocked her fingers, putting her back to the fence. Todd stepped on to her palms and clambered noisily over the top. Queenie scrambled up after him, using the gaps in the wire as hand- and toe-holds, and dropped down on the other side.

'Where now?' Todd asked.

Queenie looked around. The nearby bushes and thorny knots of grass were just black shapes against the grey ground. It was impossible to tell where the undulating landscape ended and the sky began. Over in the distance, a spotlight beam tracked across the sky. Queenie couldn't judge the distance, but there was a good chance if they walked in any other direction they'd find themselves in the middle of an uninhabited desert, where the only human contact would come in the form of sun-bleached skeletons.

'That way,' Queenie said.

Todd looked over at the distant beam of light.

'It looks a long way,' he said.

Queenie scowled. 'Do you want to get out of here or not? At least we know there's civilization in that direction.'

She heard Todd sigh and rub his arms.

'Well, I suppose we'd better start walking.'

They set off with their hands thrust deep into their pockets. Every so often an invisible branch would trip one of them up, and Queenie would cuss like a drunken pirate while Todd muttered something about the dire lack of serviceable footpaths, but otherwise they didn't talk. Queenie began to hum, to maintain the silence as much as to break it. She wasn't quite sure what someone like her might say to someone like Todd; he sounded like he'd been raised by Mary Poppins. It was hard to imagine how he'd ever become embroiled in something as dangerous as this. *He'd never even climbed a fence before!*

Queenie suddenly realized that Todd wasn't beside her. She turned to find him standing a few paces away.

'What?' she asked.

'Were you just humming "A Spoonful of Sugar" from *Mary Poppins*?' he asked.

Queenie was glad it was too dark for him to see the colour rush to her cheeks.

'No! Now come on – I don't want to spend all night out here.'

And so they trudged on in silence. With the swathe of stars above and the cold darkness pressing all around, it felt like they were walking through deep space, or crossing the barren plain of some long-dead planet. It was a glimpse of Earth's future, a hundred years or a thousand years or a million years from now.

The silence grew so heavy that eventually Todd had to say something. He looked up at the Mac-Tonic™ moon and swallowed involuntarily.

'Did you mean what you said back there?' he asked. 'Do you really know the Mac-Tonic™ formula?'

Queenie kept her eyes on the beam of light. She'd forgotten she'd said that about the recipe. She wanted to deny it, but that seemed a bit pointless now.

'Yes.'

They walked for another minute before Todd said, 'How?'

Queenie sighed. 'It washed up in a bottle near my house.' She knew it was the kind of anecdote that required more of an explanation, but she didn't feel like talking about it. She changed the subject. 'You said there was someone else with you in that room – before me. What happened to them?'

Todd didn't reply immediately, and Queenie wondered whether she'd asked something insensitive.

But then Todd said, 'I don't know what happened to him.'

They walked on in silence for a while.

'What was his name?' Queenie asked, eventually. And eventually, Todd replied, 'The Kennedy Kid.'

They walked for hours without reaching the spotlight, but it grew steadily bolder. Queenie worried that someone might turn it off, causing them to lose their bearings, but it swept the sky all night long, and only began to fade with the lightening dawn. By that point, they were almost there.

They came to another chain-link fence, not far from a chained and padlocked gate. This time, Todd boosted Queenie over first, and he followed afterwards. When they were both on the other side, Queenie looked back and saw a collection of red and white warning signs fastened to the gate. They all carried messages like RESTRICTED AREA and WARNING and NO TRESPASSING, without actually revealing what the danger on the other side was. Queenie gazed at the town – more a scattering of wooden houses and corrugated sheds – and narrowed her eyes.

'I know this place,' she said.

Todd raised his eyebrows.

'What?'

It was the most forgettable place he'd ever seen.

Queenie's mind was reaching back to the stacks of well-thumbed paperbacks her uncle had left behind. The musty, warped tomes had described this place: some had even contained grainy black and white photographs. She squinted into the pale morning light, and spotted something she'd thought was part of an outbuilding.

But it wasn't an outbuilding.

It was a 30-foot alien.

'Oh my God,' she said, looking back at the chain-link fence that disappeared into the distance. 'This is Area 51.'

Mad Theories

'Area 51? Are you sure?'

'Todd, there's a 30-foot sculpture of an alien over there.'

Todd squinted, and then raised his eyebrows.

'So there is . . .' He looked over his shoulder at the assortment of warning signs fixed to the fence. 'I thought Area 51 was where the government tested top-secret aircraft and did alien autopsies?'

'So did I.'

Queenie shivered at the memory of the underground complex, but beneath the terror there was a thrill of excitement. She had escaped – not just Area 51, but North Nitch and her humdrum life – and the feeling was so delicious her shiver turned into a full-body shudder. She could go anywhere, she could do anything, she could be anyone! She just had to keep moving.

'Come on, let's get away from this fence.'

They made their way towards the assortment of buildings by the highway. Queenie was tired and thirsty and desperately wanted a Mac-Tonic™. She knew a sweet coffee would have to do. But when they reached the roadside diner it was still closed. They made their way from place to place – a motel, a gift shop, a gas station, a gift shop, a gas station, a motel – but everywhere was still asleep. Each establishment had a kitsch UFO-inspired name, like E.T. ETC. – GIFTS AND SOUVENIRS and THE OUTER SPACE INN. Tourist tat abounded. There were little green men everywhere, with spindly limbs and big heads and black, almond-shaped eyes. Not real ones, of course: just models and murals and stickers and posters and billboards and key rings and toys. Up close, they saw that the 30-foot statue was made from battered sheets of tinplate that had been bolted together by someone who clearly didn't get many commissions to build statues of 30-foot aliens. It looked better from afar. Behind it, they found the searchlight rocking back and forth on well-oiled hinges. Queenie wondered if it ever stopped, or whether it was left to project its beam all day, invisible in the brilliant blueness of the vast Nevada sky.

They walked until they reached a scattering of rundown houses at the edge of town. They stared along the highway. The morning was already hot, and the heat haze made the road look like it led straight into a lake.

'Well,' Queenie said, 'this place sucks.'

'Yep. What do you think we should do?'

'*We?*' Queenie peered at Todd. 'Are you suggesting that we stick together?'

Todd blushed. 'I just thought that . . . well . . . we'd stand a better chance together. They always split up in movies, and it never ends well.'

'Why don't you just go home? It's me they want.'

Todd scratched his head and looked back at the desolate little town.

'I'm stranded in the middle of the desert with no money: I don't think going home is an option right now. Besides, they'll only hunt me down again. I might not know the recipe, but now I know someone who does. That's more than I knew the first time they kidnapped me. They'll take me just to get to you. And I'm a talker – I'll tell them whatever they want to hear. I mean it.'

It was hard to argue with that.

'Fine,' Queenie said. 'But I'm leaving you behind if you slow me down.'

'I won't,' Todd said.

'We'll see.'

They both looked along the blistering highway.

'We can't stay here,' Queenie said. 'They'll come looking for us the moment they realize we're missing. They might already know.'

'We can't exactly walk to the next town, though, can we?'

'No.'

'Maybe we could hitchhike?'

Queenie looked along the empty road. 'I think you need passing traffic to do that.'

They both looked around for some kind of solution. That's when Queenie realized they were being watched. Her eyes snapped back to the road.

'Don't look now, but there's a woman with long white hair watching us from her porch.'

Of course, Todd looked right away. Queenie was already beginning to doubt how long she could evade capture with Todd in tow. He was about as subtle as the Grand Canyon.

'She's calling us over,' he whispered. 'What do we do?'

Queenie looked back at the white-haired woman. There was no mistaking it: she was beckoning them with a crooked finger like they were Hansel and Gretel.

'Well,' Queenie said. 'I guess we'd better go meet the neighbourhood. Just let me do the talking, all right? And stop looking so shifty.'

They walked over the dusty plot and climbed the porch steps. The woman rocked gently in her chair, watching them from the corners of her eyes. She somehow looked suspicious and amused at the same time.

'You kids weren't thinking of walking out of town, were you?'

'No, ma'am,' Queenie said.

'Good, because the next town's forty miles away. You'd be deader than roadkill before you were halfway there.' She continued to rock in her chair. 'You're not from round here.'

It wasn't a question, and it wasn't like Queenie could have denied it if even if it had been. There were only half a dozen houses in the town.

'No, ma'am. I'm from Nebraska.'

Queenie was already imagining the search party, asking around to see if anyone had met a girl from Kansas. She hoped Todd had that in mind, too.

'Never been,' said the woman. 'What about your friend? Does he talk?'

Queenie looked at Todd. He looked unsure how to proceed for the best, but eventually mumbled, 'Yes, ma'am.'

'And from where do you hail?'

Todd shifted on the spot. 'All over, really. My family moved around a lot.'

'Figures,' the old woman said, looking out at the empty road and the desiccated land beyond. 'You've got a nowhere accent. You sound British.'

'My mom is from England. I went to school there for a bit when I was younger.'

That explains the Mary Poppins vibe, thought Queenie.

The woman nodded. There was a long silence. Queenie was beginning to wonder whether this was a normal exchange in small-town Nevada. It was less of a conversation and more of an interview. She wondered what she had to say to pass.

'I'm Cassandra,' the woman said abruptly, as though she'd just been asked. 'What should I call you?'

'I'm Gracie,' Queenie said, before Todd had a chance to answer.

'I'm John,' Todd said.

At least he's not a complete dunce, Queenie thought.

Cassandra nodded like a sage, and continued to rock. Out on the highway, a car came into view. The sound of its engine carried across the emptiness. Cassandra watched it approach and pass with interest. Queenie was about to thank Cassandra for her time and drag Todd as far away from this place as possible when the woman turned her head and fixed them with her pale eyes.

'Well, Gracie. John. Aren't you going to tell me what you were doing on government property?'

Queenie froze.

'Excuse me?' she said.

A faint smile played at the corner of Cassandra's mouth, like she was dealing with a toddler who was denying all knowledge of the missing brownies through chocolate-smeared lips.

'I saw you climb over that fence,' she said, pointing a long, slender finger over one shoulder. 'I've seen plenty of people try to get in, but in all my time I've never seen anyone come out.'

Queenie opened her mouth to explain – completely unacquainted with whatever would tumble out – but Cassandra raised a finger.

'I know what goes on in there, and I know it's not

pretty.' She levered herself out of the rocking chair. 'I think you'd better step inside.'

Cassandra shuffled into the house. Queenie and Todd spotted a circle of aluminium foil on the back of her head, like a skull-cap.

They looked at each other. They looked out at the endless desert, the empty road. It was already 80 degrees.

'I guess we don't really have a choice,' Todd said.

'I guess not.'

So in they went.

It was dark in the little house, and stuffy. The shutters were closed. Dark wallpaper with an inconsistent pattern added to the oppressive atmosphere. The couches were covered in tasselled maroon throws, and the low table in the centre of the room held so many scraps of paper that sheets were continually slipping from the pile on to the floor, like chunks falling from an iceberg.

Cassandra was standing in the far corner, in a little kitchenette that was open to the sitting room. In the opposite corner an open doorway revealed an immaculately tidy bedroom. It was the only other room. The bathroom must have been out back. It was, like everywhere else Queenie had been since her abduction,

165

somehow worse than her ramshackle house in North Nitch. It was almost enough to make her homesick.

She wondered what had become of Ma and Chuckie following her abduction, and couldn't escape a vision of them happily drinking Delixir™, oblivious to her disappearance.

'Do you two want a drink?' Cassandra asked.

Queenie and Todd were wary of consuming anything this woman had to offer, but as they were pretty much dying of thirst, they said yes. Queenie crossed her trembling fingers in the desperate hope that this strange old lady had a stockpile of Mac-Tonic™ hidden away somewhere.

'Water OK?'

Damn!

'Yes, ma'am,' they said in unison.

Cassandra took three enamel mugs from a shelf and dipped them in a tub by the cooker. She came over with her fingers looped through the handles, dripping water on to the bare floorboards, and handed out the cups. The water looked clear, and didn't smell of anything, so Queenie and Todd gulped it down. It tasted delicious, in the way only thirst-quenching, life-saving water can.

'I get my water brought down from Montana,' Cassandra said. 'The rain gets caught in wooden barrels, sealed and put straight on the truck. If the government thinks I'm drinking their tainted tap water they've got another think coming.' Cassandra saw the puzzled looks on her guests' faces and tapped her nose. 'It was lead in the pipes that finished the Romans off, you know?'

Queenie didn't know where to start. Todd did.

'Why don't you just drink bottled water? There's a store across the road.'

'Poisoned.'

There seemed to be no further explanation required. Queenie had just about found her tongue.

'Who brings you water all the way from Montana?' she asked.

'Someone I trust. Now, sit down and let's get properly acquainted.'

As they moved towards the couches in the centre of the room, Queenie noticed that the walls seemed to fidget and stir. She sat down and squinted in the gloom. At first, she thought it might be a hallucinatory side effect of her Mac-Tonic™ withdrawal. But then she saw that the walls weren't covered in dreary wallpaper, like she'd first thought, but instead were plastered with newspaper cuttings.

She looked down at the empty enamel mug in her hands and wondered when the sedatives or stimulants or hallucinogens – or whatever this woman was on – would kick in.

Queenie and Todd sat together, their backs to the door. Cassandra sat opposite them, on the far side of the table covered in paper. Queenie tried to read a couple of the pages, but everything seemed to be written in code.

'Why don't we start with your real names?' Cassandra said.

Queenie and Todd exchanged a guilty glance.

'Don't worry, I don't blame you. It's always a wise move, in my opinion. But I can tell a Kansan from a Nebraskan when I hear one, although I suspect you've spent some time in the Golden State. That, or you watch too much TV. And you, *John*, are probably the worst liar I have ever encountered. The tips of your ears go pink when you lie. If you're planning to make a habit of it, you might want to consider investing in some earmuffs.'

The two fugitives looked at their knees. Eventually, Queenie opened her mouth to respond, but Cassandra leaned forwards and silenced her with a finger.

'Put these on first,' she said, reaching under the table to retrieve two aluminium foil hats. They were clearly homemade. Queenie wondered whether it was possible for aluminium foil hats to be anything other than homemade. (She was yet to venture inside E.T. ETC. – GIFTS AND SOUVENIRS, which sold a mesmerizing variety of telepathy and mind-control deterrents.)

'Are these really necessary?' Todd asked.

'Yes,' said Cassandra. 'If you knew what I knew, you'd wear one all the time.'

Reluctantly, Queenie and Todd donned their shiny hats. Queenie did not look at Todd, and Todd did not look at Queenie. It was an unspoken pact.

'You two aren't carrying any kind of electronic device, are you? Nothing capable of transmitting a signal?'

They both shook their heads. The foil hats rustled against their hair.

'Didn't think so. I'm highly sensitive to electromagnetic radiation so I can normally tell. Besides, I'm guessing if you came from over the fence they took anything like that off you.'

Despite serious misgivings about her host, Queenie was curious to learn the shape of Cassandra's madness. Years of reading science fiction novels by oddballs with overactive imaginations had left her with a keen sympathy for weird folk.

'What do you know about Area 51?' she asked.

'Names first,' Cassandra said.

'Queenie.'

'Todd.'

Cassandra sat back and smiled. 'You want to know what goes on inside Area 51?'

Queenie nodded.

'Well, contrary to what most people think, Area 51 is not a facility for testing secret weapons or cutting up aliens. Although God alone knows why an alien race capable of journeying to Earth from a distant galaxy would choose to visit Nevada. There have got to be better places in the universe to run out of fuel.'

Amen to that, Queenie thought. *Time to find out what even crazier theory she's cooked up in this cabin.*

'Area 51 isn't even a *government* facility. It's privately co-owned by two of the dastardliest companies in the history of the world: The Mac-Tonic™ Corporation and Delixir™ Enterprises.'

Queenie's jaw went slack. Todd's eyes widened. Between them, in their aluminium foil hats, they were the picture of vacuous, mind-controlled alien slaves.

'People think the secret military projects are a cover

story for the alien autopsies, but the alien autopsies are cover for what really goes on in there.'

'And what does go on in there?' Queenie asked.

'Do you still doubt me?' Cassandra replied. She flapped a hand in the vague direction of the papered walls. 'I've been on to them for decades. That place is a den of iniquity! It looks innocuous enough from the outside – just a featureless, one-storey building – but it goes ten storeys *down*. It's like an iceberg: most of it is hidden beneath the surface.'

Queenie and Todd thought of their subterranean cell.

'Do you want to know why it's called Area 51?' Cassandra continued. 'It's a joke. When Mac-Tonic™ and Delixir™ went in on this, Mac-Tonic™ insisted on paying for fifty-one per cent of the project. They can't tolerate anything less than a majority share.'

'But . . . but Mac-Tonic™ and Delixir™ wouldn't co-own anything,' Todd said, his voice panicky. 'They hate each other!'

'That's all just for show. What's good for one is good for the other. They're thick as thieves, make no mistake.'

This was really pushing the limits of what Queenie was willing to believe. She looked at Cassandra: a faint sheen of sweat glistened on the old woman's forehead.

The whites of her eyes were visible around the edges of her pale irises.

'But why do they both use the same space?' Queenie asked. 'What could they both have in common?'

'Secrets and enemies,' Cassandra hissed. 'The upper levels are where their enemies – people who have got on the wrong side of Mac-Tonic™ and Delixir™ – are brought in for questioning. But I'm guessing you two know all about that already.'

'What kinds of people?' Todd asked. His voice shook. He looked unwell. Queenie wondered whether he was thinking about his own experiences over the past fortnight.

'Come on,' Cassandra said, getting up. 'I'll show you.'

Queenie and Todd followed Cassandra to one of the walls, where she lifted a piece of newspaper to reveal another sheet below.

'Back in the 80s, Mac-Tonic™ introduced an artificial sweetener that had some pretty serious side effects: dizziness, blindness, hallucinations – that kind of thing. One mother decided to sue the company after her three sons staggered off a cliff near the family home. She claimed they'd all been drinking Mac-Tonic™. Naturally, Mac-Tonic™ didn't want this to get out, so they didn't let it.'

Queenie and Todd read the clipping. It was only small, and the dense text was impossible to read in the low light, but the headline was clear enough:

MAC-TONIC™ PLAINTIFF FAILS TO ATTEND
HEARING – CASE THROWN OUT

'What happened to her?' Queenie asked.

Cassandra let the top sheet fall back over the clipping. 'She's a long-term resident of Area 51.' Cassandra moved along the wall, pointing out different stories as she went. 'There was the dentist who campaigned against the ruinous effects of soda on children's teeth; and McGregor Coulson, the Olympic athlete, who identified the soda giants as the main culprits behind the obesity epidemic; and Reginald Clancy Holmes, the senator, who tried to implement a nationwide sugar tax on fizzy drinks. All of them disappeared under mysterious circumstances; all of them now live in Area 51. Most of the subterranean floors are given over to prison cells.'

'What about the ones that aren't?' Queenie asked, tearing her gaze away from the endless newspaper cuttings. 'You said some are used for questioning, but what are the other levels used for?'

Cassandra lifted a hand and pointed to a miniscule cutting that was golden with age. Queenie and Todd moved closer.

NEWLY RETIRED DELIXIR™ BOSS
BECOMES RECLUSE

There was another cutting below it.

FORMER MAC-TONIC™ EXEC ATTEMPTS
ROUND-THE-WORLD SOLO TRIP

The clipping beneath was dated several months later.

MAC-TONIC™ EXEC YACHT STILL
MISSING – SEARCH ABANDONED

And there were several more: reports of retired executives taking up dangerous pursuits, or shunning public life in favour of a remote cabin in an undisclosed location, or just plain vanishing. Spaced apart by years or even decades, as the stories were, the trend must have been easy to miss. But seeing them all together, separated by only a thin margin of decaying paper, the pattern was impossible to ignore.

'They do it to their own?' Queenie asked.

Cassandra nodded.

'The bottom floor of the building is given over to executives who know part of the secret formula and have retired or tried to move to another company. That floor is really quite luxurious, even if it is ten storeys below ground.'

'And Delixir™ does it too?' Todd asked.

'I can see you're still having trouble viewing them as two sides of the same coin, but yes, Delixir™ does it too. Their secrets might not be quite as valuable, but they're still worth hundreds of billions of dollars.'

'But if they're kept in the same building,' Todd said, 'couldn't they give their company's secrets away to their competitors? What if they got out somehow?'

'You don't understand,' Cassandra said. 'The executives can't share their secrets because they can't remember them. Shortly after they arrive, they're lobotomized. There's no remembering your own name after that. Besides, *nobody* gets out.'

Todd looked decidedly ill.

'But we got out,' Queenie said. 'And it wasn't even that hard.'

Cassandra shrugged. 'If you escaped, it must be because they wanted you to escape.'

Queenie was disappointed. She'd been beginning to view Cassandra less like a lunatic and more like a prophet. It was clear that their improbable escape didn't fit her theory, and as a result her explanation wasn't really an explanation at all.

'How do you know all this?' she asked.

Cassandra had started to read a front page from the 1930s with the headline: *MAC-TONIC™ CONTINUES TO PROSPER DESPITE GREAT DEPRESSION*. And, even though she turned back to Queenie immediately, her expression seemed faraway, as though she was still thinking about the article.

'I know all this because I'm the architect who designed Area 51.'

Queenie wasn't expecting that. It nearly knocked her foil hat off.

'I didn't know what it was for at the time – all they said was that it was a government contract, and I assumed like everyone else still does that they would be using it to develop top-secret projects. When I found out its true purpose I kept it to myself; I knew what would happen if I spoke out. I think they planned to detain me anyway and so, towards the end of the project, I went into hiding.'

'If that's true, why haven't they hunted you down?' Queenie asked. 'And why do you live so close to it?'

'So I can keep an eye on them, of course!'

Cassandra suddenly looked like she'd been wired to the mains: she was charged with a dangerous energy. She jumped a few notches up Queenie's crazy scale.

'And they *are* still looking for me! Why do you think I wear this hat, and live like the Amish? They're on to me! The last time I went to a built-up area, black helicopters started following me around!'

Queenie's heart tripped on the doormat. 'Black helicopters?'

'Have you seen them too?' Cassandra's eyes were close to popping out of their sockets. 'Did you see them on your way here?'

'No,' Queenie said. 'Back in California. There were three of them.'

'*Three!* What on earth did you do to get three on your tail? What do you know?' She threw up a hand and turned her head away like a nervous horse. 'Don't tell me! If I don't know, they won't be able to get it out of me. They're sure to come here now.' She ran to the window and peered out of the shutters.

The thing about paranoia is that it's contagious: it can make even the most rational person suspicious. Out in the middle of nowhere, in a dark room filled with the evidence of a lifetime's misgivings, in the company of someone completely unhinged, pretty much anyone will start to believe pretty much anything. Queenie was on dangerous ground, and it was dangerous precisely because she shared it with a madwoman. They had both been stalked by black helicopters, and there weren't many people outside of the asylums – or Area 51 – who could claim that. Queenie felt a sudden need for the company of someone who wasn't certifiably insane.

She turned to Todd, and was disconcerted to find him on the far side of the room, fixated on a particular newspaper clipping. He seemed a terribly long way away.

'I don't get it,' he said, frowning at the wall of headlines. 'There are articles here that have nothing to do with Mac-Tonic™ or Delixir™.'

Cassandra's head snapped round to where Todd was standing. 'Like what?'

'Well, this one here for a start.'

Queenie and Cassandra followed his gaze to a front page that was legible even from the opposite side of the room.

KENNEDY ASSASSINATED

'Oh, that,' Cassandra said dismissively. 'Mac-Tonic™ were behind that.'

Queenie decided right there and then that Cassandra was out of her mind, but instead of making her cautious it made her angry.

'And why the hell would Mac-Tonic™ want to kill the President?'

Cassandra didn't seem to notice the scorn in Queenie's voice. She sounded, for once, quite reasonable.

'The space programme wasn't progressing as fast as Mac-Tonic™ would have liked. They held Kennedy responsible. They needed astronautical superiority in order to implement their Lunar Projection System – the technology that beams their logo on to the moon – so they made sure the space race became the government's top priority. The LPS programme is still coordinated from the observatory at Hard Labor Creek, if memory serves.'

Queenie shook her head in dismay. They really needed to get out of here soon. It had been almost twenty-four hours since she'd consumed anything sweet or caffeinated and she was beginning to feel extremely jittery. Weakness seeped through her body with every heartbeat: it felt as though someone had pulled a stopper somewhere, and the lifeblood was pumping out of her. Queenie felt sure that if they didn't leave soon, she would faint.

'Sit down,' Cassandra said, observing Queenie's wooziness. 'I'll get you some more water.'

But Queenie did not sit down. She stood and swayed on the spot. It felt like she was losing her identity. Every square inch of wall space was covered with newspaper cuttings – sometimes two or three sheets deep – and each one detailed a global disaster or personal tragedy spanning the last century.

And her beloved Mac-Tonic™ was behind them all.

'I think we'd better be going now,' she said.

Her voice was flat and trancelike and, although it unsettled Todd, Cassandra did not seem surprised. She leaned in closer to Queenie.

'You know, you can tell me the formula if you like?'

Queenie looked up but Cassandra suddenly didn't seem close enough to have whispered the words.

'What?' Queenie asked.

Cassandra smiled. 'I said, let me give you a few dollars for the road.' She fetched a brown envelope from a drawer in the sideboard and took out one hundred dollars in well-worn bills. She gave half to Todd and half to Queenie. 'Just in case you get separated.'

Queenie nodded dumbly.

'Now,' Cassandra said, 'here's what you're going to do.'

Queenie poured a heap of sugar into her coffee, stirred it and gulped it down. The coffee wasn't particularly hot, but the bitterness of it made her cough. The bottom of her mug was lined with an amber slush of half-dissolved sugar, and she spooned it into her mouth like dessert. Todd watched the whole thing with fascination, his hands gripping the edge of the table.

'I get the shakes,' Queenie admitted, glancing around the empty diner. 'Ever since the Mac-Tonic™ ran out I've had to find things to replace it with.' She poured herself another cup of coffee and added more sugar. She was just about to take a sip when she noticed Todd's glass of juice.

'How did you get over Mac-Tonic™?'

'Oh.' Todd sipped his juice through a straw. 'I've never really liked it.'

Queenie's face fell, and Todd stared down into his glass. His immunity to Mac-Tonic™ never failed to garner disbelief and disapproval.

'So why didn't you order a Delixir™?'

Todd slowly stirred his juice. 'I don't drink that either.'

Queenie had heard some pretty strange stuff in the past hour, but someone who didn't drink Mac-Tonic™ or Delixir™ was right up there with anything Cassandra had to offer. She drank her coffee in two fortifying gulps.

'I know,' Todd said, turning his attention to the approaching waitress. 'It's weird.'

You can say that again, Queenie thought.

The waitress placed their breakfasts on the table – Queenie had ordered pancakes with all the extras, while Todd had gone for the Solar System Breakfast – and they tucked in. It was the greatest meal of Queenie's life. Her stomach twisted and groaned in excruciating delight with every forkful of buttery, syrupy batter. The stack was about nine inches high. It made Queenie want to stand on her seat and shout, 'God bless America!'

They were supposed to be looking out for a truck with *Harvey's* on the side – a truck that Cassandra had promised would take them far away from this place – but for ten minutes they were too distracted by their food.

Eventually, after another cup of sugary coffee, Queenie began to feel human again. Todd mopped the last of the yolk and grease and bean sauce from his plate with a piece of bread and sat back, stuffed. A familiar, uncomfortable silence settled between them.

'So,' Todd said.

Queenie kept her eyes trained on the gas station across the road. 'So . . .'

The awkward silence stretched. Queenie considered asking Todd something about himself, or the family that he hadn't seen for two weeks, but she wasn't sure she wanted him to ask the same questions about her, so she kept quiet. She scraped the last of the sugary slush from the bottom of her cup and spooned it into her mouth. Todd stared out of the window – clearly he didn't think they had anything in common either.

Finally, Queenie dropped her spoon into the mug with a clatter.

'What do you think?' she asked. 'About what Cassandra said?'

'I don't believe it,' Todd said, shaking his head. 'I can't believe it.'

'Don't you think any of what she said might be true?'

Todd sipped his juice while he thought about it. He looked troubled, like he suspected it might be true, but wanted it all to be a lie.

'No,' he said, eventually. 'I think she's a paranoid old lady who's lived alone for too long. That foil hat must have fried her brain.'

'But she knew about Area 51,' Queenie said, lowering her voice. 'About what goes on in there.'

'But Mac-Tonic™ and Delixir™ working together? It just doesn't make sense. It's unthinkable. And what about all that other stuff – the conspiracies and assassinations? They can't be that . . . evil.'

But he didn't sound so sure.

'What are we going to do when this truck shows up?' Queenie asked, her voice little more than a whisper.

'Let's just see if it turns up first.'

They both looked out of the window and saw a truck pull into the gas station across the road. It had one word on its side: *Harvey's*.

A balding man with a halo of black hair jumped down and stretched his legs. Queenie and Todd watched as Cassandra appeared at the roadside and scurried across. She was still wearing her aluminium foil skull-cap.

'Everything all right for you?' the waitress asked.

Queenie and Todd turned around with a start.

'Great,' Todd said.

'Anything else?' the waitress asked.

'No, thanks.'

She collected their plates, put the bill down between them and left. By the time they looked back out the window, Cassandra was gone. The truck driver was staring at their booth from across the road.

'I guess we don't have much choice,' Todd said.

'Are you sure you want to come with me?' Queenie asked. 'You've got some money now, and I'm sure they'd let you use the phone here to call your parents or nanny or whatever.'

'Nanny?'

'Look, all I'm saying is you don't have to do this. It's me they want.'

Todd shook his head. 'They won't stop until they capture us both, so we may as well stick together.'

'To make it easy for them?'

'No, to make it difficult.' Todd smiled hopefully. 'You never know, I might come in useful.'

Queenie rolled her eyes. 'Stranger things have happened, I guess. Come on. Let's go.'

She left enough money on the table to cover the food and a tip and together they left. They crossed the road and stood in front of the truck driver, who introduced himself gruffly as Bill. Queenie got the impression that Bill wasn't much of a conversationalist – that perhaps he chose to drive trucks long distance in order to restrict the amount of time he had to spend in the company of other human beings. He looked at Queenie and Todd with undisguised loathing. Finally, he spat on the ground and thrust his hands deep into his pockets.

'It's gonna be a long ride. I'm not stopping unless I need to, so go get whatever you need from the store and be back here in five minutes.'

Queenie and Todd did not wait to be told twice. They headed towards the store.

'And make sure you pee if you gotta pee!'

It was a relief to be inside the store, if only because they were separated from Bill by a sheet of glass.

'I'd say it's going to be a *very* long ride,' Queenie said. 'I'll buy some snacks.'

'OK, I'm going to use the bathroom. Meet you by the truck.'

Queenie walked up and down the aisles, piling potato chips and candy bars and bottles of allegedly poisoned water in her arms.

The cashier was a young man in a washed-out yellow shirt, with a shaving rash beneath his chin and bloodshot eyes. At the checkout, he rang through each item as though he knew they would be added to his very own shopping cart in hell. Like the waitress who'd served them in the diner, he woke up each morning wondering what he'd done to deserve such an insipid existence. If only God would answer his prayers and bestow a great gift upon him. Then, perhaps, he could escape this small town in the desert and make something of his life.

'Eleven sixty-five,' he said.

When the robots finally take over, they'll be hard pressed to find a more monotonous voice to use.

The girl across the counter didn't seem to be paying attention. She was too busy watching the TV hanging from the ceiling behind him. And if only he'd turned around to look at what she was watching, he'd have seen that God was trying to answer his prayers.

Because Queenie was looking at a picture of herself. And beneath the image was a scrolling banner that read:

--- MISSING: QUEENIE DE LA CRUZ ---
$10 MILLION REWARD --- CALL MAC-TONIC™
HOTLINE WITH INFO NOW ---

'Hey, miss,' the cashier said. 'Do you want this stuff or not?'

Queenie's attention drifted back to the man in front of her.

'Yeah,' she said. 'Sorry. How much?'

'Eleven sixty-five.'

Queenie fumbled with her money and thrust a five and a ten at the cashier.

'Keep the change,' she said, scooping up her shopping and hurrying out of the store. She didn't look back.

Out on the forecourt, Bill turned the key in the ignition and the truck rumbled into life. Todd was waiting by the open door on the passenger side.

'Look what I got next door,' he said, holding up a grey backpack shaped like an alien's face. 'Couldn't resist. I thought we could use it to carry our supplies.'

He noticed Queenie's drawn face and put out a hand to stop her from climbing up.

'Are you all right?' he asked.

She nodded, swallowing hard.

'Are you two coming or what?' Bill hollered, over the noise of the engine.

'Let's just get out of here,' Queenie said.

She climbed up, and Todd clambered up after her. He shut the door, and the truck pulled out on to the empty highway.

Back in the store, the cashier counted out $3.35 in change and slipped it into his pocket. *Maybe things are looking up*, he thought. *Maybe there is a god listening to my prayers, after all.*

12

The Best Pie in Texas

Earl McLaughlin wiped the grease from his mouth with the back of his hand and stared up at the screen. Bruce Dillinger's manic face smiled back.

'It's day fifteen of the Great Thirst, folks, and if the Death-o-Meter is anything to go by, people are really starting to feel the pinch. We just passed the two thousand-casualty milestone and the carnage does not look like stopping any time soon!'

'You or your friend want anything else, sweetie? We got some of the best pie in Texas. Don't let that man on the TV put you off.'

Earl McLaughlin turned away from the TV screen and looked at the waitress. She had a little gold-coloured name badge that read: DOLLY. Then he turned to look at his brother, sitting on the other side of the red plastic table.

'What do you say, Cody? Fancy a slice of the best pie in Texas?'

Cody stopped picking at the stringy bacon fat between his teeth and slid his eyes on to the waitress.

'I would love a slice of the best pie in Texas.' He grinned. 'What flavours have you got, Dolly?'

'Most fruits you can think of, but we're famous for our gooseberry. And my name's not Dolly; Dolly's the name of a girl who quit two years ago. The manager's too cheap to buy new badges.'

Cody put the toothpick back in his mouth.

'So what is your name?'

The waitress was used to talking to all kinds of people – she served dozens of customers every day – but there was something about the two men sitting before her, so at ease in their odiousness, that scrambled her usual, superficial breeziness. They exuded violence and cruelty and meanness. She glanced out of the window and knew immediately which vehicle was theirs: a dusty black pickup with plates she didn't recognize. She wished she had her glasses on, so she could read the registration, but her manager had banned her from wearing them because he thought they made her look serious. *Too intelligent*, he'd said at the time.

She regretted telling them that her name wasn't really Dolly. Most days, she viewed her tarnished, hand-me-down nametag as a blessing. It gave her a persona with which to absorb the petty humiliations.

'My name's Karen,' she said.

This was not her real name. She suspected that the two men knew this.

'Well, *Karen*,' Cody said, 'I would most definitely like a slice of your famous gooseberry pie.'

She wrote it down on her pad.

'You want ice cream with that?'

Cody nodded, so that she had to look up from her pad to find out.

'And for you?'

Earl puckered his lips and drummed his fingers on the tabletop.

'The best pie in Texas, you say?'

Karen nodded. 'That's what it says above the door.'

'Well, I'll hold you to that.' He made it sound like a threat. 'Put me down for a piece.'

She knew that he knew there was an optional side of ice cream, but he still made her ask the question.

'You want ice cream with that?'

'You betcha, Karen. I want it all.'

Karen was desperate to walk away, but she was also

gripped by a sudden conviction that if she did these men would be the last two she ever saw. She needed to demonstrate that she knew all about their evil schemes.

'You two aren't from round here, are you?' she asked.

'No. No, we're not from round here, Karen. Just passin' through.' Earl tilted his scarred head to one side. 'What makes you ask?'

'You sound different, is all.' She pointed her pen at the black pickup in the parking lot. 'Is that your vehicle?'

Both men turned slightly to see which vehicle she was pointing to.

'Yep,' Earl said, turning back. 'That's us.'

'Is that a New Mexico plate?' she asked.

She knew it definitely wasn't a New Mexico plate, but she wanted to see whether they would lie to her about it.

'No,' Earl said, with a generous smile. 'They're Louisiana plates. That's where we're from. *Louisiana*.'

She was sure he knew why she was asking the question. She was sure that they'd known from the moment they set off on their murderous adventure that she would be here, and that she would lie about her name, and that she would try to reassure herself that she wasn't about to become their next victim by trying to learn something about them – by asking about their registration plates. It was all part of their plan.

'You ever been to Louisiana?' Cody asked.

She shook her head.

'You wanna visit sometime?'

'No,' she managed to say. 'No, thank you.'

Cody shrugged. 'Your loss, *Dolly*.'

She took two steps back before turning and hurrying to the kitchen.

'You reckon that pie is gonna be as good as she says?' Cody asked, glancing at his brother.

Earl gave him a doleful look. 'I reckon it was bought at a store and is bein' zapped in a microwave as we speak.'

'That's too bad,' Cody said.

They both turned back to the TV hanging behind the counter. Bruce Dillinger was still holding the fort with undiminished enthusiasm.

'We've got a caller on the line who thinks he has information on the missing Mexican girl, Queenie de la Cruz. What's your name, sir?'

'Karl. Karl Winterson.'

'Good afternoon, Karl. The line's a bit patchy. Where are you calling from?'

'Nevada. Just outside Area 51. I just told someone all this already.'

'Ooh, spooky. Have you seen any UFOs lately?'

'No. Not once. Now, how do I get the ten million dollars?'

'Well, have you found the Mexican girl?'

'She was here this morning! I'm sure it was her!'

'And is she there now?'

'No, of course not! She left about four hours ago. Do you know anybody who hangs around a gas station for more than ten minutes?'

'I'm guessing you might be one of those people, Karl.'

'Ha ha.'

'So, tell me what happened this morning.'

Karl sighed heavily. He'd just explained everything to someone screening the calls.

'She was in here this morning about nine. She bought a pile of potato chips and candy, like she was stocking up for a long journey. I'm sure it was her! I'd bet my life on it!'

Bruce Dillinger leaned in, with one elbow resting on the desk, the way he'd seen serious journalists do on other channels and in the movies. He frowned. He associated the posture with words like veracity, and credibility, and integrity, without really understanding what any of them meant.

'Why do you remember this so well, Karl?'

'Because she left more than three dollars in change! Nobody ever tipped me like that before.'

'And was she alone, Karl?'

'No, she wasn't. Hang on, I'm just rewinding the tape.'

'You caught her on tape?'

'I said hang on!'

There was a pause that was filled with the whirring of a decrepit VCR machine and the muttered cussing of Karl Winterson.

'There she is!' he suddenly exclaimed.

'Can you describe what she was wearing?'

'Jeans. Pale jeans and a dark T-shirt.'

'And was she alone?'

'No, there was a boy out by the pumps. They got into a truck with *Harvey's* on the side. Looks like they headed south on US 93. Now, when do I get my ten million dollars?'

'I'm afraid that reward is for whoever finds Queenie de la Cruz.' A smile broke across Bruce Dillinger's face. 'It sounds like what you've had is a . . . *close encounter*.'

Karl Winterson did not appreciate the joke. He cursed Bruce Dillinger in the most colourful language he could think of before slamming the phone down.

The smile slid from Bruce Dillinger's face, like a dead bird down a windowpane.

'You still there, Karl? Karl?' He raised his eyebrows. 'I guess not. We're joined now by an expert in fugitive thinking, Dennis Rednall. Dennis, what do you think is going through this girl's mind right now?'

Dennis' credentials as an expert in fugitive thinking were pretty watertight: he was a fugitive himself.

'Well, it's clear to me that this Mexican girl is heading to the states with the highest Hispanic populations so she can blend in and avoid detection: New Mexico, Arizona, Texas. Once she's there, it'll be like finding a needle in a haystack.'

'This no longer seems to be a search for a missing person,' Bruce Dillinger said, with impeccable insight. 'This situation has developed into a manhunt, wouldn't you say? Or a *girl*hunt, perhaps?'

Bruce Dillinger really was on fire today.

'Come on,' Earl said, grabbing his combat jacket from the seat beside him. 'Time to go.'

The McLaughlin brothers got up from their table and headed out into the sweltering afternoon sunshine.

Karen was on her way to their table with two plates of gooseberry pie when she saw them striding across the parking lot. She reached their table and found that they hadn't left any money for the food.

This is their plan, Karen thought. They wanted her to follow them outside, demanding payment for the meal, so they could throw her in the back of the truck and speed off before anyone knew what had happened. She'd be dead before sunset.

She stood by their table and watched as the pickup pulled out of the parking lot and accelerated on to the highway. She watched until it was lost in the heat haze. The two scoops of ice cream melted against the deep slices of gooseberry pie. Then she took the pie back to the kitchen.

She paid the McLaughlins' bill from her own pocket. It was better than having anything further to do with them.

Pitchforks and Flaming Torches

Queenie crossed her legs and prayed that Bill would stop at the next gas station. He'd been drinking coffee from a giant flask all morning, but it seemed his bladder had the capacity of a Great Lake. When midday came and went, Queenie began to wonder whether he had a urinary catheter strapped to his calf.

Finally, he pulled in at a truck stop and Queenie leaped down before they even came to a halt. She found a bathroom and nearly cried with the relief. It was a disgusting place, with a wet floor and obscene graffiti all over the stalls, but she didn't care. She would have left a glowing review on her way out if they'd had a guestbook by the door.

She found Todd stretching his legs by the truck. Bill was nowhere to be seen.

'How long have we been on the road?' Todd asked. He'd slept most of the way.

'About four hours. I needed a pee for three and a half of those.'

'Good to know.' He looked around at the parked trucks. 'Where are we?'

Queenie shrugged. 'We must be somewhere in Arizona by now.'

'Do you know where Bill's going?'

'No. Bill's not much of a talker.'

The cab was still full of junk food and bottled water, but Queenie needed something to take the edge off her cravings. She was beginning to itch.

'Do you want another coffee?' Todd asked.

'You read my mind. It's got to be better than standing around here waiting for Bill.'

They wandered over to a coffee place that was sandwiched between two fast food restaurants.

'Were you telling the truth earlier?' Todd asked. 'Have you really been followed by black helicopters?'

Queenie nodded.

'I'm all over TV too. I saw myself in the gas station this morning.' She glanced at Todd. 'You should probably know there's a ten-million-dollar bounty on my head.'

Todd puffed his cheeks out. 'I guess the coffees are on you then.' He smiled, and Queenie was annoyed to find herself smiling too.

He may be a liability, she thought, *but at least he's got a sense of humour.*

They reached the coffee place. It was pretty much identical to its ten thousand sister restaurants across the country. They joined the queue.

'What can I get you?' the cashier asked, without looking up.

'Two black coffees, please,' Todd said.

'You want to go grande for an extra 60 cents?'

'OK.'

'Anything else?'

'No, thanks.'

'Seven dollars and thirty cents.'

Todd handed over the money. The cashier gave him his change. Then she took a pen and made marks on the side of two cups.

'Names?' she said.

'John,' Todd said.

'Queenie,' Queenie said, at the same time, without thinking. She was too distracted by the promise of a highly caffeinated sugar hit. The cashier didn't seem to notice. The panic ebbed out of Queenie's heart.

'Pretty name,' she said.

She scribbled on the side of each cup, and added a little doodle of a crown instead of doting the 'i' above Queenie's name.

'They'll be ready in just a minute.'

She finally looked up, and her retail smile faltered. There was a flicker of recognition, but then it passed. There were people waiting, after all. Time is money.

'Who's next?' she asked.

Queenie stepped away from the counter and sat on a stool by the window. Todd remained standing. He glanced over his shoulder every few seconds.

'What's our plan?' he asked. 'Do we have one?'

Queenie huffed. Her foot bounced on the rung of the stool.

'Maybe I should just turn myself in? If you did it, you'd get ten million dollars. Maybe we could split the money?'

Todd shook his head. 'And risk being sent back to Area 51? No way. Besides, what if the things Cassandra told us are true? What if Mac-Tonic™ was behind all those disappearances and assassinations? What if Delixir™ is in on it too?'

'I thought you didn't believe a word Cassandra said?'

'I don't know. I'm not sure what to think any more. But if there's a chance that Mac-Tonic™ and Delixir™ are half as bad as Cassandra says, then we need to keep ourselves – and the recipe – out of their hands.'

Queenie didn't know what to say. She was annoyed that she still craved an ice-cold glass of Mac-Tonic™, even while she suspected it might have fuelled most of the atrocities committed in the past century. She had Lyle Funderburk and the boys in Marketing to thank for that.

Something outside suddenly caught her eye.

'Is that Bill?'

Todd looked up and swore under his breath. Bill was striding away from the row of storefronts, glancing about in every direction. He walked so fast he was almost jogging. As he neared a bank of payphones he delved into a pocket and spilled coins all over the ground. He bent down and picked up enough coins to make a phone call. The rest he left glistening in the sun.

'It looks like Bill just found out how precious his cargo really is,' Todd said.

'Damn,' Queenie said. 'We need to leave. Just slip away before anyone realizes we're here.'

A loud voice drawled over by the counter.

'Two Americanos for John and . . . Queenie!'

A cold sensation swept over Queenie, and it had nothing to do with the air conditioning vent directly above her head. The whole coffee place went quiet. People started looking around. Queenie kept her face turned to the window. Bill was talking now, waving his hands excitedly.

'I'll get the coffees,' Todd muttered. 'Meet me outside.'

Queenie slid from her stool and pushed through the glass door. She stood in the stifling Arizona sun with her back to the coffee place. She wanted to run, but she knew it would be a mistake. At any moment, she expected a heavy hand to land on her shoulder and drag her away.

The door behind her swung open with a gust of cold air.

'Start walking,' Todd said, handing her a coffee and heading across the parking lot.

'What happened?' she asked.

'They're suspicious. I expect half of them are M-T™ addicts trying to take the edge off with coffee. There was an ugly atmosphere. We need to disappear. Come on, let's head for the truck and get our stuff.'

They walked across the vast parking lot without looking back. As soon as they reached the truck bays they began to weave between the parked vehicles. Queenie hung back while Todd went up to Bill's truck, opened the door and stuffed the snacks and water into his alien backpack. He closed the door with his elbow.

'Come on,' he said. 'I think I heard raised voices.'

Queenie could hear them now as well. 'We need to hide.'

'Start checking the doors on some of these trucks.'

They continued to weave between the vehicles, stopping at the back of each one to see if it would open.

'No good,' Queenie said, rattling yet another locked door.

The voices were either getting louder or getting closer, or both. For some reason, Queenie imagined the mob with pitchforks and flaming torches.

'What about that one?' Todd asked.

He nodded in the direction of a smaller van, with a white shutter drawn down at the rear. Queenie ran forwards and saw there was no padlock. She threw it open and peered inside. It was full of strawberry punnets.

Todd let out a short laugh. 'Could be worse,' he said, dumping his backpack beside a stack of crates. 'It's kind of our only option.'

They both clambered up and dragged the shutter down. It was very dark, and Queenie felt a packet of potato chips pop and crunch beneath her foot as she tried to find a place to sit. Outside, it sounded as though a full-blown riot was underway.

'How long do you think we're going to have to hide in here?' Queenie asked.

Todd's breathing was loud beside her. 'As long as it takes for things to die down.'

Queenie sipped her coffee. 'Ugh. Didn't you put any sugar in it?'

'I was kind of preoccupied. You'll just have to eat some candy every time you take a sip.'

Queenie shot Todd a look he couldn't see, but then she took his advice and fumbled around for some candy. Slowly, the itch began to fade.

They'd both just finished their coffees when a voice shouted close by – closer than all the others – and a moment later the van rumbled into life.

'Looks like we're on the move,' Todd said. 'I wonder where we're headed now.'

'Probably best to hold on to something.'

They both grabbed one of the nearby stacks and braced their feet against another. The van took off with a lurch. It snaked from one side to the other, trying to escape the carnage of the truck stop. The engine roared as the driver accelerated, and the sounds of the skirmish quickly faded into the distance.

As the van joined the highway, Queenie and Todd heard the thudding blades of an approaching helicopter.

'Probably just a news chopper,' Todd said.

'Probably,' Queenie replied.

14

A National State of Emergency

'I'm telling you,' Randy van de Velde said. 'She don't wanna be found!'

He jabbed his finger against General Sherman, leaving a smudge on the table's polished surface.

'But that doesn't make any sense,' Alexander Greenberg said. 'Why would she not want to be found? We've already established that she drinks an above average amount of Mac-Tonic™; she should be as impatient to get it back on the shelves as anybody.'

'Beats me,' said Randy van de Velde. 'I've never understood Mexicans.'

The board had given up trying to disabuse Randy van de Velde of the belief that Queenie hailed from Mexico long ago.

'It doesn't matter why,' Dwight Eagleman said quietly. He fiddled with the cufflink on his right sleeve, as though that was the thing most deserving of his attention. 'What's important is that she's found. I think we need to revise our strategy.'

'But we've only just finalized the copy for a nationwide billboard campaign,' Donnie Holland said. '*God Save Our Queenie*, remember?'

'Scrap it,' Dwight Eagleman said.

Donnie Holland knew better than to push his luck. 'So what's the line now?'

Dwight Eagleman, satisfied with the positioning of his cufflinks, stood up. He leaned forwards, pushing both palms on to the table, and looked around the room.

'Think about what this girl is doing. She's withholding the formula to the greatest beverage the world has ever known. She is depriving billions of people of what is rightfully theirs and turning neighbours against one another. The people are angry, and right now, they are angry with us. The Mac-Tonic™ Corporation. What we need to do is turn that anger on Queenie de la Cruz.'

He straightened up, and everyone knew better than to speak now. Dwight Eagleman was like a gathering storm – there was nothing you could do about it but watch.

'The time has come to mobilize the people. We're going to denounce and demonize Queenie de la Cruz.

We're going to make sure everyone knows her name and is repulsed by it. I don't want her to be able to come within spitting distance of another human being and not be spat at. We need to foster hatred and suspicion and vengeance. She is a fugitive, she is a criminal, and she is an enemy to anyone who values this great country. She is no longer a missing person, she is now a *wanted* person. I'll contact the President personally and ask him to declare a national state of emergency.'

'You could get him to fly the flag upside down above the White House,' Donnie Holland suggested. 'Give the campaign a striking visual that will really resonate internationally.'

There was muttered agreement. Dwight Eagleman's eyes were suddenly ablaze.

'That's good,' he said. 'I need our best copywriters on this, Donnie. Oversee everything. The campaign needs to be clear but subtle. Play on the Mexican angle – stir up some old prejudices. Maybe put the suggestion out there that she's an illegal. But temper the whole thing – don't forgot that she's the only person who knows the formula. The last thing we need is some nut taking her out before we've got the recipe back. Nothing goes without my approval, understood?'

Donnie Holland nodded. The disappointment of the aborted *God Save Our Queenie* campaign was already forgotten. This would be his magnum opus, a masterclass in psychological manipulation. He was going to turn hundreds of millions of people into witch-hunters, and he was going to stop them just short of igniting the pyre.

Silvio Rizzuto cocked his head to one side.

'What are we going to do when we finally catch her?'

All eyes turned to Dwight Eagleman, like gladiators waiting for the emperor's verdict.

'We will ensure that she is punished to the full extent of the law.'

'Naturally, but what will she be charged with?' Silvio Rizzuto asked. 'There's no doubt a crime has been committed, but what is her crime? Can we even accuse her of theft if she *found* the formula?'

This time, all eyes turned to Alexander Greenberg. The lawyer made a steeple with his fingertips while he contemplated the legalities of their predicament. He was still for a long time, but then he levered himself up out of his chair and strolled over to the wall that was adorned with Mac-Tonic™ bottles. He reached up to one of the earliest designs – a thick-glassed affair with a swing-top stopper – and took it down. Inside, eighty-year-old Mac-Tonic™ sloshed into the stubby neck.

'You're right,' he said, turning back to the board. 'Proving theft would be tricky. She found the formula, fair and square. But what did it wash up in?'

The question was rhetorical, but Randy van de Velde had always struggled with rhetorical questions.

'A Mac-Tonic™ bottle!'

'Exactly. And what did we stop printing on Mac-Tonic™ labels in 1967?'

Randy van de Velde didn't know the answer to that one. He was stumped, as was everyone else in the boardroom. Except Dwight Eagleman. A knowing smile crept on to his face. Alexander Greenberg began to stroll back and forth in a leisurely manner.

'1967, gentlemen, was the year we stopped printing "Property of The Mac-Tonic™ Corporation" on our labels, following the decision to phase out our bottle-return scheme and move to single-use packaging.'

He held the antique bottle before them, like a waiter presenting a bottle of fine wine. Sure enough, printed along one edge of the diamond-shaped label were the words: *Property of The Mac-Tonic™ Corporation*.

'You can no longer find these words on our products, but legal ownership of each and every Mac-Tonic™ receptacle remains with us. Ergo, unless Queenie de la Cruz can prove she bought the particular bottle that washed up near her home – which I sincerely doubt she could – legal ownership of the bottle, *and its contents*, reverts to The Mac-Tonic™ Corporation.'

There was an awed silence. Sometimes, if you rarely found yourself in a courtroom with him, it was easy to forget just how skilled a lawyer Alexander Greenberg was. He had never lost a suit. He had crushed every imitator and competitor, repelled every attack on the Mac-Tonic™ brand. The corporation had only suffered one legal defeat, back in 1991, when the courts had ruled that it could no longer use the word 'miracle' in its branding or advertising. Use of Macfarlane's Miracle Tonic™ had been in decline anyway, but it was still an unprecedented loss. The lawyer who presented the case against Mac-Tonic™ all those years ago was a young, fresh-faced attorney called Alexander Greenberg. Mac-Tonic™ acquired his services the following week, and the very next month he argued successfully for a reversal of the ruling.

Some guys just know how to win an argument.

'We are sure to win on the charge of larceny. However, I don't think we should limit the reach of our case to petty theft.'

Alexander Greenberg replaced the vintage bottle of Mac-Tonic™ with great care. He turned to face his colleagues.

'I think we should strive for a more . . . resounding conviction: an outcome that befits the true crime being committed here. After all, millions of people are going to be bitterly disappointed if this little girl ends up with a slap on the wrist and a few months' probation.'

He paused. It was, undoubtedly, a meaningful pause.

'Our case rests on whether we can convince a court that our product is intrinsically American. Is Mac-Tonic™ woven into the fabric of American culture? Does Horatio Macfarlane's story epitomize the American Dream? Would America be America without Mac-Tonic™? I'm confident that I could make the case that our product is, in fact, quintessentially American.'

'What are you getting at here, Al?' Randy van de Velde said.

Alexander Greenberg smiled a rueful smile.

'I think we should contest that Queenie de la Cruz has committed treason.'

There were disbelieving stares, but the lawyer pushed on.

'If Mac-Tonic™ is a symbol of America, if it embodies American ideals and is beloved by the American people, surely a deliberate action to harm it – to destroy it – must be deemed a treasonous act.'

'What's the penalty for treason?' Martin DeWitt asked.

'It depends on the jurisdiction, but this crime originated in California, and in California the penalty is death or life imprisonment without parole. I would make a point of seeking the death penalty. It would be a fitting end to the ordeal, don't you think?'

Donnie Holland nodded with especial enthusiasm. The whole case had a wonderful narrative arc and he knew, just as well as Alexander Greenberg, that criminal cases were as much about telling a great story as any piece of evidence.

Alexander Greenberg looked to Dwight Eagleman for his blessing.

'You're sure you could win this case?' Dwight Eagleman asked.

Alexander Greenberg held his gaze. 'Absolutely. Whip the people up into a frenzy and there won't be a single judge in the land willing to rule against us. Besides, at least half the jurors will be Mac-Tonic™ drinkers, and I think we can be pretty sure of their verdict before the trial even begins.'

Dwight Eagleman nodded.

'Well, gentlemen. Let's go find Queenie de la Cruz.'

Moon-gazers

The van finally came to a stop. The cab door opened and slammed shut with enough force to rock the vehicle and wake Queenie up. Todd's hand covered her mouth immediately. Someone approached the side of the van and spat on the ground.

Queenie and Todd waited. They expected the shutter to fly open at any moment and, although they were hidden behind a stack of crates, it wouldn't take the driver long to find them if he started unloading his cargo. There was the sound of scuffed footsteps, of grit being crushed beneath soles, of passing traffic.

Queenie wondered whether the driver was armed.

But then the footsteps receded. Queenie and Todd waited a few minutes before crawling towards the shutter and lifting it up. Queenie poked her head out and looked around the near-empty parking lot of a diner. It was late evening. Some of the cars out on the highway already had their lights on, and some didn't.

'Quick,' she said. 'Before someone spots us.'

'Hang on,' Todd said. 'Let me just grab the trash.'

'Why?' Queenie asked, just a voice escaped from the labyrinth of her memories.

It's your world too.

Todd jumped down with a handful of empty wrappers and punnets.

'To cover our tracks.'

'OK,' Queenie said, picking up their coffee cups and throwing them in the nearest trash can. 'Can we get out of here now?'

Todd pulled the shutter down, glanced around and joined Queenie on the side of the van that shielded them from the diner.

'What now?' Todd asked. 'Where are we?'

Queenie peered at the registration plates of a couple of cars parked nearby.

'It looks like we're in New Mexico, which means we're heading east. That's good. The sun is setting over there, so we need to head in the opposite direction.'

'But how?' Todd asked. 'Maybe we should get back in the van and see where we end up?'

Queenie shook her head. 'I'm pretty sure the next stop the driver makes will be for a delivery, and then he'll find us. How long can you keep strawberries in an unrefrigerated van, after all?'

'So what do you suggest?'

'Hitchhike?'

'And get picked up by the cops? Cassandra told us we couldn't trust them, remember?'

'Well, we're just going to have to take a chance. I'm not spending the rest of my life here!'

She looked around the forlorn parking lot. She was beginning to think America might be just one big network of highways joining gas stations and diners and motels with thousands of other gas stations and diners and motels. A constant stream of vehicles rushed by on the highway, and she wondered whether any of the drivers had homes to go to, or if they just criss-crossed the country, stopping every now and then to rest and refuel, before resuming their endless, pointless journeys.

It felt like a long time since she'd last seen North Nitch, and the pang of longing in her chest was so sharp and unexpected it made her gasp.

'You OK?' Todd asked.

'Fine,' Queenie replied. She had a sudden urge to be alone. 'Why don't you head into that diner and see what they're showing on TV? There's a chance there might be someone here who's been on the road all day and hasn't seen the news and doesn't know what I look like. Maybe we could get a lift from them?'

'Good idea.'

'I'll wait out here.'

Todd walked away and Queenie sat on the bank of earth between the parking lot and the highway. She watched Todd until he reached the door to the diner, but then she lost sight of him. In her mind, she ran through the Mac-Tonic™ recipe. It was incredible to think she was the only person on the planet who knew the ingredients to something that almost everybody on the planet had tasted. She looked to the sky, hoping to see the Mac-Tonic™ moon, but it hadn't yet risen. At one point she struggled to remember one of the flavourings and felt a stab of panic in her chest. But when she ran through the list again it came back to her, and the panic trickled away.

But the knowledge began to weigh down on her. She didn't know if it was stress or tiredness or the days of sugar and caffeine withdrawal, but she was beginning to wonder whether she actually wanted another taste of Mac-Tonic™. What if Cassandra's ravings and ramblings were founded on truth? What if, in its quest for global domination, The Mac-Tonic™ Corporation had done despicable things?

Then again, what if none of it was true? Mac-Tonic™ had sent people to her house with a generous reward for finding the formula, after all. It wasn't like they had tried to take it by force. What if she was keeping billions of people from enjoying one of life's simple, affordable pleasures? And what was she even planning to do with the recipe? She couldn't run for ever – could she?

'Good news,' Todd said.

Queenie flinched. 'What is it?'

'They've got a game on TV, and I saw a guy in there wearing a Rangers cap.'

'So?'

'So he probably comes from Texas. If he's heading that way we could catch a ride with him. Let's hope the Rangers win.'

'Why?'

Todd sighed. 'Because I'm guessing he'll be more likely to give us a ride if he's in a good mood.' He sat down beside Queenie. 'All we have to do now is wait.'

And wait they did. The moon rose, and they watched as a few people shuffled out of the diner to stare up at it. Queenie had heard about these so-called moon-gazers back in North Nitch – people who spent hours just staring at the Mac-Tonic™ logo, trying to imagine the taste of it on their tongues once more. There was something unspeakably sad about them: looking to a barren world when their own was so rich and wild and full. The tragedy of it – and the realization that she could easily have become one of them – crushed Queenie's resolve, forcing tears to her eyes. The Mac-Tonic™ moon fractured into a kaleidoscope of red and white slivers.

I can't do this on my own, she thought. *I can't hold up the moon.*

She wiped her eyes and took a deep breath that did nothing to calm her nerves. Instead, it only made her realize how much her body was shaking.

'Todd.'

Todd was lying back on the bank with his hands behind his head. 'Mmm?'

'I want to tell you the formula.'

Todd sat up straight. 'What?'

'The formula. I want to share it with you.'

Even in the darkness, Queenie could see the puzzled expression on Todd's face.

'Why?'

'Because I'm worried something is going to happen to me, and it will be lost for ever. And because if you're going through this with me, it seems only fair.' She paused and rubbed her hands on her shins. 'And because it's too much for one person to carry.'

They were quiet for a while. The passing cars threw white light on one cheek and red on the other.

'Only if you're sure,' Todd said, eventually.

Queenie nodded.

And then she told him.

And then there were two people on planet Earth who knew its greatest secret.

'There he is,' Todd said. 'That's him.'

They watched the man cross the parking lot. He seemed a little unsteady on his feet.

'Is he . . . drunk?' Queenie asked.

'Maybe a little,' Todd said. 'But we can't stay here all night. Come on.'

They got up and intercepted the man just before he reached his car.

'Hey there,' Todd said, with a friendly wave. 'Did we win?'

The man looked up and smiled. He was skinny and unshaven and not at all stable.

'You betcha! What a game!'

'I can't believe we missed it. We had tickets and everything, but our car broke down and we've had no luck getting a ride back to Dallas.'

The man opened his arms wide.

'Well, jump in. I'm not going as far as Dallas but I'll get you most of the way there.'

'You don't mind?' Queenie asked.

'Not at all. The more the merrier.'

He opened the passenger door and bowed like a chauffeur, then made his way round to the driver's side using the car as a crutch. Queenie and Todd exchanged a glance.

'You should go in the back,' Todd muttered. 'He's more likely to get a good look at you if you're sitting beside him.'

Queenie got into the back, and Todd climbed into the passenger seat. They both fastened their seatbelts.

'What are your names, kids?'

'I'm John, and that's my sister Gracie in the back.'

'Nice to meet y'all. I'm Melvin, but feel free to call me Melvin.'

Todd turned to look at Queenie.

'Thanks, Melvin,' they said.

'I said call me Mel! I insist!'

He started the ignition, and a woman's voice came blaring out of the car radio.

'. . . *increasingly clear these eco-warriors will not back down without concessions from government and industry, and each day more and more people are joining the protests at various locations across—*'

'Boring!' Melvin shouted, switching the radio off. 'Now, off we go.'

The car smelled of sweet beery breath before they even exited the parking lot. Joining the highway was one of the most terrifying experiences of Queenie and Todd's short lives. Queenie thought they would have caused less commotion if they'd been in a shopping cart. She probably would have felt safer too. But Melvin seemed oblivious to the honking horns as he meandered from one lane to another and back again, while he explained the minutiae of every inning. The odometer was fixed at 90 miles per hour.

It was a relief when they left the highway and joined a quieter road. The landscape was black and empty. They could have been driving on the ocean floor if it wasn't for Melvin's open window, which he'd presumably wound down to sober himself up. Every so often they passed an isolated house with the American flag flying upside down on a pole out front, but otherwise there was no sign of human habitation for miles and miles.

Todd fell asleep in the front seat. His head lolled against the headrest. Queenie had slept in the back of the van but only fitfully, and the monotonous drive and sudden drop in adrenaline were making her sleepy. She knew at least one of them needed to stay awake, but sometimes sleep is a folding wave you just can't resist. It dragged her under, and rolled her around, and pulled her deeper.

Queenie woke with a start. Blearily, she became aware of an insistent tapping noise, as though one of the tyres had blown out. She remembered where she was and who was driving and how drunk he had been in a rush of fear. She became convinced that she was listening to the wheels pass over the rumble strips and off the road. She focused on Melvin, expecting to find him asleep at the wheel, but found him very much awake. The drumming noise was being made by his thumbs on the steering wheel.

It was bright in the car and Queenie squinted against the glare of the interior light. She couldn't understand why it was on. Maybe Melvin had been searching for something and in his drunkenness had forgotten to switch it off?

Queenie looked into the rear-view mirror and saw that Melvin was watching her closely. He didn't seem embarrassed to be caught watching her. Occasionally his eyes darted back to the road, but only for a moment. Queenie tried to see where they were or where they were headed, but the interior light made it impossible. The windows had become mirrors; the windscreen reflected her face.

'What did you say your name was again?' Melvin asked.

Adrenaline pumped around Queenie's body, heightening her awareness.

'Gracie,' Queenie replied. 'Where are we?'

Melvin didn't reply. His eyes flicked to the road. Flicked back to the mirror. They were bloodshot.

'And you say you two are brother and sister?'

'That's right,' Queenie said. Her mind was scrambling for information, but all she had was the fusty, littered car, illuminated by the interior light and reflected back by the windows. 'John is a year older than me.'

She raised her voice slightly, hoping it would wake Todd, but he slept right through.

The bloodshot eyes darted sideways, then back to the mirror.

'You don't look much alike.'

Queenie's heart was pounding like a caffeine hit at bedtime. She tried to keep her voice casual, bored. She imagined she was talking about Chuckie and felt unexpectedly homesick. It's amazing what being tired and strung out and two time zones apart can do to someone's sensibilities.

'John takes after our pa, I take after Mom.'

Melvin's eyes were pretty much fixed to the little mirror. He regarded the road now and then, as though it was a painting that wouldn't change. Queenie glanced down at the empty bottles of Mac-Tonic™ by her feet and wondered when his last taste had been. Judging by the crazed look in his eye, it had been some time.

'And you were on your way to the ball game tonight?'

'What?'

'The ball game,' Melvin repeated. 'He said you had tickets to see the Rangers.'

'Oh, we did.'

'Show me.'

'Show you what?'

'The tickets!'

Todd was stirring.

'John had them. He ripped them up when we knew we were going to miss it. He's got quite a temper,' she added, as an afterthought.

'You don't sound Texan,' Melvin said.

'That's because I didn't grow up in Texas.'

'Where did you grow up?'

'Why are you asking?'

'Because I want to know! It's my car, and I've got a right to know who I'm transporting.'

Melvin hadn't looked at the road for almost half a minute. It was beginning to pose a bigger threat than any of his questions. But then Queenie saw headlights up ahead, and prayed that it might be a highway patrol car. She couldn't think of anyone else who would be driving at this time. If she could just keep Melvin focused on her for a few more seconds, the officer would hopefully get suspicious about the interior light being left on and pull them over. Cassandra's warning about the police would just have to wait.

'We're from Nebraska, originally, but we moved around a lot.'

She held Melvin's stare. The headlights drew closer.

'All right then, tell me this. Who's your favourite Rangers player?'

Queenie's eyes darted to Todd. He was blinking.

'John's the one who likes going to games. I just get dragged along.'

'Don't lie to me!' Melvin said.

He suddenly spotted the approaching car and must have had the same thought as Queenie, because he snapped the interior light off and gripped the steering wheel hard. Queenie's heart sank. She'd caught a glimpse of the oncoming vehicle and it wasn't a patrol car: it was a pickup truck. It zipped past the window in a flash of black and chrome.

But something strange had happened. All the reflections in the windscreen had disappeared the moment the light was switched off. Except for one.

Her own.

Queenie leaned forwards and squinted through the glass. Todd was awake and staring at it too, so she knew she wasn't hallucinating. Up ahead, suspended above the horizon, was the moon. But instead of the Mac-Tonic™ logo, a different image was being projected: Queenie's face. The word WANTED hung over the image, and beneath her chin were the words: $10 MILLION REWARD.

Melvin chuckled.

'Well, Miss de la Cruz, you look like you've seen a ghost.'

She couldn't speak. She was struggling to breathe. She looked around frantically.

'Just sit still now. I've got no intention of slowing down to let you out. In fact . . .' He delved into a pocket and fought to bring out his cell phone. 'I might just call for backup. In case y'all get any ideas.'

Todd glanced at Queenie, and his horrified face mirrored hers. But then his eyes widened, and a pale light illuminated his face.

'Hold on!' he said.

The car lurched and swerved as something rammed into the back of it. Queenie's seatbelt dug into her neck.

'Goddamnit!' Melvin shouted, reaching into the footwell to retrieve his phone.

An engine surged and a black pickup raced past them. As soon as it was ahead of the car, it moved over to straddle both lanes.

'Who the hell are these guys?' Melvin asked.

Queenie watched a man clamber halfway out of the passenger window. He turned to face them. He raised an arm.

'Get down!' Todd shouted.

Queenie ducked behind the driver's seat as a hole was blown in the windscreen. Cool air rushed in and the car began to swerve sickeningly from side to side.

'Oh my God!' Todd shouted. 'Hang on!'

The car left the road and hit the low bank of earth like a ramp. It corkscrewed through the air, throwing crumbs of glass and Mac-Tonic™ bottles around the interior, before landing on its roof with a crunch.

The wheels kept spinning. The undercarriage hissed. Something dripped.

Nobody got out.

16

Chum

For the second time in as many days, Queenie found herself tied up in the back of a moving vehicle. It was pitch-black. The road roared beneath her. She had no idea how long she had been unconscious. It was unbearably hot, so she guessed it must be daytime. But which day it was, and in what year, she had no way of knowing.

A piece of cloth dug into the corners of her mouth, making it impossible to cry out. She was desperately thirsty. The vehicle turned sharply and she slid into something softer than a wall. It groaned. Her heart fluttered with the knowledge that she wasn't in this situation alone. Todd was here. She lowered her cheek against the hard, gritty floor and closed her eyes.

'Wakey-wakey, boys and girls!'

The brightness was blinding. Queenie closed her eyes and felt someone fumbling with the rope around her wrists. Her limbs unfurled painfully as soon as they were released. She rolled on to her back and peered into the glare. Two silhouettes loomed over her.

'Who are you?' Queenie asked.

'It don't matter who we are,' one of them said. 'It's who *you* are that's important.'

Queenie sat up, expecting the men to stop her, but they didn't. She was in the back of a pickup truck. One of them, a large man with a cigarette clamped between his lips, was tying back the tarpaulin behind the driver's cab. The other, sinewy and scarred and bald as an egg, stood with his dirty hands clasping the gate. A shotgun dangled from a strap on his shoulder. He smiled, but it felt like being spat at.

'Now, listen up, Queenie de la Cruz. I'm about to ask you a very important question. Where we're goin', there ain't no room for passengers.' He took out a large serrated knife from a sheath on his belt. He pointed it at Todd, who was still bound on the floor of the pickup. 'I don't know who this boy is, but I do know he don't have a ten-million-dollar bounty on his head.' He stared at Queenie, as though he'd asked her a question. She stared at the knife. The blade was made from a dull brushed metal that didn't catch the sun. 'I'm lookin' for a reason not to chop him up and toss him to the alligators.'

Queenie's fear of unseen alligators was conquered by her fear for Todd. She would have said whatever these men wanted to hear, if only she knew which words to say.

'Well, is he worth takin' or not?'

'Yes,' Queenie said, her voice desperate.

'She's lyin', Earl,' the bigger man said, leaning over to prod Todd in the ribs. 'The only thing this one's good for is chum.'

'Shut it, Cody,' Earl said. He turned back to Queenie. 'What makes your boyfriend so special?'

Queenie looked down at Todd. The skin around his wrists was red raw, and his T-shirt clung to his back as though someone had doused him with a bucket of water. He tried to say something through his gag, but it just came out as a panicky mumble.

'He knows the formula too,' Queenie said.

Earl raised his eyebrows, rucking the skin of his swarthy forehead.

'Is that so?'

'I still say she's lyin',' Cody said, emptying Todd's backpack and downing a bottle of water.

'Well, there's only one way to find out.'

Earl reached into the truck and severed the ropes. Todd wrenched the gag away from his mouth and gasped. Before he could speak, Cody had him by the neck and was forcing him out of the truck. Queenie scampered out after him. Cody threw the empty backpack at Todd, who caught it and slung it over his shoulder, and moved closer to Queenie. Earl flicked his knife towards the water, and they both followed.

'What happened to Melvin?' Todd asked under his breath.

Queenie didn't dare think about what had become of their driver. She glanced around, searching for some trace of him, but the marshy river mouth was deserted.

The McLaughlin brothers led them down to a decrepit jetty, where a black boat was moored. A gun was fixed at the stern, above the motor, and it looked like something that had been amputated from a tank. An ammunition belt hung down and folded into itself on the floor like warm syrup. There was a structured harness and stirrups. It was the kind of weapon that made you wonder what kind of trouble you were likely to run into out on the water.

Queenie and Todd sat on the floor of the boat. Earl stood over them on the jetty while Cody trudged back to the pickup. He returned a few moments later with a black metal box in one hand and a grenade launcher in the other. The boat bobbed precariously as the brothers climbed in. Cody sat beside the motor, and Earl stood in the bow, behind the steering wheel.

'Where are you taking us?' Todd asked.

Earl looked over his shoulder and smiled.

'Last Island,' he said. 'You're gonna love it.'

The boat sped away from the jetty. The engine was too loud to talk over, but Queenie wasn't sure what they would have talked about even if it were possible. She looked back at the receding shore as they bounced across the waves. There were no signs of civilization: just a few broken sheds and jetties and floating Mac-Tonic™ bottles. If they were where she suspected they were, a hurricane probably swept through every year or so, obliterating everything. People had obviously given up trying to live here. It was yet another place that was, somehow, worse than North Nitch.

The boat bounced along at speed. Queenie's dark hair wrapped around her face and trailed behind. It was like being blindfolded. Todd kept his eyes on the floor of the boat, which was littered with wet cigarette butts. He had a bad feeling about this trip. It didn't seem like a trip that many people would embark on voluntarily, and he wasn't sure whether it was a trip from which they were likely to return.

A belt of scraggy islands came into view. They sat so low in the water that the boat was almost upon them before Queenie noticed. A medium-sized swell would probably have submerged the whole chain. The highest point was barely taller than a man. It was crowned with a little makeshift shed, and it was to this shed that the boat was headed.

Earl pulled alongside another battered jetty and Cody moored up.

'Out,' Earl said.

Queenie and Todd stepped out and were shoved up a short flight of warped steps to the shed. It was made from driftwood and planks from old boats and sheets of corrugated metal and blue tarpaulin. There was nothing inside. Absolutely nothing. Not even a chair or a lantern or a dead seabird.

Queenie and Todd stood in the centre of the room. It was hotter than a pizza oven. Earl and Cody followed them inside and pulled the door shut, which seemed unnecessary to Queenie: the nearest person must have been miles away. Cody carried the metal box over to the far corner and set it down. He took off his combat jacket and let it drop to the floor. His vest was a collage of stains and discolourations. Then he knelt by the box and opened it up.

Inside was a collection of implements. They looked like the kind of tools a dentist might use, back when dentistry was a sideline for bloodthirsty barbers. Earl leaned against the wall, beside the door.

'It's been a helluva long drive to pick you two up, and Cody has been itchin' to use his box of tricks the whole time. I'm the only one who can stop him. Unless I get what I want, I don't intend to.'

Cody straightened up. There was a rusty hacksaw in his hand.

'You both know the formula?' Earl asked.

Queenie nodded. Beads of sweat scurried between her shoulder blades.

'Here's how it's gonna work. You can tell me the recipe, right here and right now, and we'll take you back without a scratch. Or, you can keep your secret bottled up inside, and Cody will break you open to find it.'

'You'll kill us either way,' Todd said, his voice wavering.

Earl scowled. 'That's not a bad idea, but I'm a man of my word.'

'You don't have to do this,' Queenie said. 'You'll get the reward just for capturing me, and you've already done that.'

Earl shook his head in that *if I've told you once I've told you a thousand times* way some people do.

'Queenie, Queenie, Queenie. How naïve you are. Mac-Tonic™ is a trillion-dollar corporation, and they're offerin' a measly ten-million-dollar reward for their greatest secret. As soon as you give me the formula, I'm gonna call up that hotline and start negotiatin'.'

'You're mad!' Todd shouted suddenly. It was panic looking for an exit: an eruption of fear. 'Don't you know what they're capable of? What they'll do to you?'

Earl stared at Todd. It was the coldest thing in the room by a long way. Then he glanced at his brother.

'I'll start with the boy,' Cody said.

He tested the sharpness of the saw's teeth with a fat thumb. It looked pretty blunt to Queenie.

'You know,' Cody said, 'they call these here parts the Dead Zone. Any ideas why?'

Queenie and Todd didn't speak. Their chests heaved up and down, up and down.

'No guesses? All right, I'll tell you. All along the Mississippi, farmers spray fertilizers on their crops to make 'em grow. Then the rains come and wash these chemicals in the river, and Old Man River carries 'em south and spits 'em into the Gulf, right here. The algae go wild, blockin' sunlight, depletin' oxygen, secretin' poisons. Everythin' else dies off. And that, boys and girls, is why they call it the Dead Zone.' He adjusted his grip on the hacksaw and smiled. 'But it ain't the only reason.'

He took a step towards Todd.

'Wait!' Queenie said. 'I'll tell you the stupid recipe!'

There was a hot silence. The shack creaked.

'Well,' Earl said. 'What are you waitin' for?'

'I need to write it down. It's kind of long.'

Earl reached into his jacket pocket and took out a stubby pencil and a piece of paper that was dirty along the folds. He passed them to Queenie.

'No messin' now,' he said, tapping the palm of his left hand with a finger. 'I'll keep you right here until this all goes through, and I can make your time with us as pleasant or as unpleasant as I choose.'

Queenie glared at him and unfolded the piece of paper. She paused. The recipe was the only leverage they had. As soon as she handed it over, the bounty hunters could do whatever they liked with them. She put the pencil to the paper. Her blood pounded in her ears.

'You hear that?' Cody said.

Is it that loud?

The thudding in Queenie's ears separated out, like there was an echo.

Earl looked at the roof, as though he could see through it. He opened the door and peered out.

'What the . . .' he said. 'How'd they find us out here? Everyone out. Come on! Out! Now!'

Queenie and Todd were hustled out of the shed and down the groaning steps. Cody shoved them into the boat and yanked it into life. The smell of gasoline filled Queenie's nostrils as Earl peeled the boat away from the jetty and headed back towards land.

Ahead of them, three black helicopters were racing across the sky.

'Buckle up!' Earl shouted above the drone of the motor. 'Cody, let 'em have it! They can't fire back while the asset's in the boat!'

Cody got behind the gun turret and threw the straps over his muscular shoulders. He turned the barrel to face the helicopters, jammed his boots into the stirrups and opened fire.

The noise was deafening, and the recoil was so fierce it forced the stern down almost to drowning point. Spent casings spun to the floor and pooled around the base of the gun. Cody was wrestling with the weapon just to keep his aim in. A manic smile was fixed on his face.

Sparks jumped from the blades of the middle helicopter, and seconds later it spiralled towards the ocean, trailing smoke and fire. It hit the water like a breaching whale. There was an almighty fizzing splash that Queenie couldn't hear, even though she was close enough to taste the spray. The other two helicopters veered wide as the boat passed beneath, before circling round in pursuit.

'Take 'em down, Cody!'

They were getting close to where they'd left the black pickup, but the boat didn't slow down. Instead, it swerved around a grassy outcrop and into the mouth of the river. Earl snaked between the marshy islands of the delta, twisting and turning and kicking up enough wash to overwhelm some of the smaller hummocks. He knew the waterways better than any boatman, and if there was anyone who could lose a couple of black helicopters in these parts it was Earl McLaughlin.

Meanwhile, the gun turret ate up the ammunition belt like a strand of deadly spaghetti.

'We just gotta get to the tree cover!' Earl shouted. 'Don't let 'em get alongside us!'

But the helicopters had already flanked the boat. Cody had to choose which one to fire at. He picked the one to the east. As he turned his back on the one to the west, its door slid open and the long barrel of a sniper rifle poked out. The boat weaved from left to right. The barrel followed it. They couldn't risk hitting the girl. The girl was everything. Over to the east, a burst of bullets punched holes in the helicopter's fuselage. It lost altitude. It landed in the dense riverside foliage and sent a fireball flooding between the tree trunks.

'Two down!' Cody shouted. He drew in a deep breath, preparing to spin the turret, and a sniper round ripped it out of him. There was a wet sound, like a Margherita pizza hitting the floor. Cody slumped in the harness, leaking all sorts of useful stuff from the wound in his chest. His hands slipped from the gun; his feet dangled in the stirrups. The golden casings took on a glossy amber sheen like treacle.

He was, as they say, out of the game.

Earl glanced over his shoulder and swore. He'd been pretty mad to begin with – he was a mad kind of guy – but seeing his brother like that pushed him to a whole new level of fury. With one hand on the wheel and one eye on the waterway, he reached down and retrieved the stubby grenade launcher from the bottom of the boat. He lifted his arm and let off several rounds, cackling like a demon. The helicopter was forced into an evasive manoeuvre as shells exploded around it. A gloved hand patted the sniper on the shoulder: he was clear to engage.

Earl twisted round to face Queenie and Todd. 'Get up here!' he shouted. 'Get up here now or we're all dead!'

The movement opened his body up to the helicopter for the briefest moment, and the sniper took his chance. The bullet passed through Earl's right shoulder, disabling his arm.

'*Goddamnit!*' he screamed.

He raised his left arm and let off a blind round. The grenade buzzed through the air like a fat bumblebee, passed over the sniper's shoulder and hit the roof of the chopper. It morphed into a ball of fire and zipping shrapnel. The black carcass fell from the sky, leaving a cloud of smoke behind like a soul.

The boat was still going full throttle, but Earl was no longer steering. By the time he dropped the grenade launcher and grabbed the wheel, landfall was imminent. He ducked behind the steering column and braced himself against it.

Queenie and Todd didn't have anything to hold on to, and so they were flung from the boat the moment it hit the marshy bank. If Queenie lost consciousness, she wasn't aware of it. The next thing she knew, she was lying on her back, looking up at the bleached sky. Her head pounded even more than before. Twenty feet away, Todd was stirring. Queenie sat up. She could see the muddy scars that their flying bodies had gouged into the earth. Beyond them, the boat was partially embedded in the riverbank. Its bow had buckled and splintered with the impact. Water poured in through the cracks. In the stern, Cody dangled from his harness like an idle puppet.

Queenie looked to her right; Todd was crawling on all fours.

'You OK?' she asked. Her throat felt sore.

'Yep,' Todd said, although it was clearly a struggle, even on hands and knees, for him to keep his balance. He reached Queenie and rolled on to his back. 'What now?'

Queenie looked around. If they were on an island, it must have been a pretty big island. The trees behind her were old and gnarled and swampy, like they'd withstood more hurricanes than any living thing had a right to. But what lay beyond them, Queenie did not know.

She opened her mouth to reply, but there was a clunk from the direction of the boat that made her freeze. Like a zombie rising from the grave, Earl clambered to his feet. The water pooling in the bottom of the boat had soaked his clothing, and it clung to his lithe body. The scars criss-crossing his scalp gleamed in the sunlight. His right arm hung limply by his side. He groaned.

Then he raised his head and stared at Queenie and Todd.

A shotgun dangled from his left hand.

It began to rise.

'Stop!' Queenie said.

She wasn't sure what she could possibly say to change Earl's mind. His brother was dead. He'd lost the use of an arm and ten million dollars to boot. As far as bad days went, it certainly put things into perspective. He held the shotgun out at arm's length. It made him look strangely lopsided.

'Wait!' Queenie said.

But she couldn't think of anything to appease him. She seemed to be articulating the only thing that could save them: delay. If she could just stall Earl long enough, he'd succumb to blood loss or shock, or the boat would sink beneath the brown water. But Earl wasn't the type to waste time. He wasn't about to describe his devious schemes and grand plans like a supervillain. In Earl's mind, the next few seconds were very simple: he was going to kill the two kids in front of him, and then he was going to die. He didn't even have a witty catchphrase.

Earl looked along the length of the barrel and closed his right eye. Even in his current state, holding the gun in his unfavoured hand, he doubted he'd need to aim too closely.

Queenie's heart hammered in her chest like it wanted to escape, like it wanted to get out of the firing line. Todd held his breath, even though he had so few breaths left to take.

Earl's finger tightened around the trigger.

And then a massive alligator ate him. The reptile launched itself on to the boat in a rush of frothy water. It must have been at least fifteen feet long, and the ridges along its powerful back glistened like spikes of cut jet. Its broad body crashed through the hull, breaking it in half, and its fat head clamped around Earl's torso. A second later, they were gone. The bow followed them beneath the surface. A few moments after that, the gun turret, with Cody strapped to it, sank to the murky riverbed.

The water stilled.

And that was the last anyone ever saw of the McLaughlin brothers.

17

Wide-eyed and White-knuckled

It turned out Queenie and Todd were not marooned on an alligator-infested island after all, but they may as well have been for all the fear and paranoia that occupied their thoughts. It felt as though their enemies surrounded them, watching from the dense foliage, waiting to strike. Queenie became convinced they were the only people who didn't know where they were. She didn't reveal her suspicions to Todd because she couldn't face being believed, just as much as she couldn't face being doubted.

The only thing they had been able to agree following the McLaughlins' demise was that they needed to put some distance between themselves and the helicopter crash sites. There could be no doubt that a fresh fleet of black helicopters was already thundering across the sky to track them down. Queenie expected an ambush with every step. She was even hoping for it. At least then it would all be over.

They waded through the thick undergrowth and between the bendy limbs of close-growing trees, sweating in the jungle heat. Queenie had never been anywhere so wild and untamed before, but gradually she came to find comfort in the claustrophobia. She'd always thought of trees growing straight up, in neatly planted rows, but the forest seemed to follow its own labyrinthine logic: growing where it could, twisting around itself, stretching for every ray of light and drop of water. There was no sign that anybody had ever set foot here before: no broken branches, no churned earth, no plastic trash. Its remoteness became a thing of safety, not fear. But it was a place that Queenie associated with the past – not the present, and definitely not the future – and she wished more than anything that it would keep unfurling before her, stretching its tendrils into the ravaged world beyond, at a rate slightly faster than walking pace.

But then, abruptly and inevitably, they reached a dirt road that lay like a scar through the forest.

And on the path, just a few feet away, lay an empty Mac-Tonic™ bottle.

Queenie glanced over her shoulder at the wilderness they had just emerged from, and already it seemed to be knitting itself together against her, as though sensing her destructive potential. And, although Queenie hadn't hacked the path or dropped the litter, she still felt to blame. She turned away, hurried after Todd and fell in step beside him.

They followed the track east, watching as their shadows grew longer on the path ahead. They walked in silence for a long time, until Todd said, 'Look.'

It took Queenie a couple of seconds to register what he'd said. She stopped and looked along the road. Up ahead, the track began to curve towards another road. At the junction stood a decrepit gas station. It looked abandoned, but there was a car on the forecourt, its windows and paintwork shining orange in the sun.

'Let's hope they have something to eat and drink,' Queenie said. 'Otherwise we may as well have jumped in after that alligator.'

She trudged on, but Todd hung back.

'What if someone recognizes you?' he asked.

Queenie didn't stop.

'I'll sign an autograph for them.'

Todd shook his head and hurried to catch up. As they approached the gas station it became apparent that no gas had been pumped there for a long time. The windows were boarded up, the pumps looked antique and the forecourt was a broken slab of concrete. A vintage Mac-Tonic™ sign hung above the door, almost rusted to illegibility, commemorating the company's seventy-fifth birthday. Todd knew Macfarlane's Miracle Tonic™ had been created in 1875, so that placed the gas station somewhere in the 1950s, which seemed about right given the general state of disrepair. It wasn't really a surprise that it had gone out of business; the strip of road beside it had been in view for almost twenty minutes, and not a single vehicle had passed by. God only knew how slow trade must have been back when cars were a luxury and not a human right.

The real surprise was the car on the forecourt. It was a red sedan, and it looked almost brand new. There wasn't a veneer of dust or a fallen leaf on it. Todd moved closer and peered through the window.

'The key's still in the ignition,' he said.

Queenie peered into the surrounding woods.

'Maybe they stopped for gas,' she said.

'Who would stop here for gas?'

Queenie shrugged. 'Someone who ran out of gas?'

Todd opened the driver's door and turned the key in the ignition. He checked the display and turned it off again. He put the key in his pocket.

'Nope,' he said. 'Tank's almost full.'

'I don't like it,' Queenie said. The paranoia was intense.

'Why don't we wait around and see if anyone comes back for it? We've got no idea where we are, or where the next town is. This could be our way out of here.'

'I still don't like it,' Queenie said.

Todd shrugged and went round to the trunk.

'There's no food or drink in here,' he said, 'but there are blankets and a torch. Why don't we sleep in the store, and if no one comes back for the car by morning we'll borrow it?'

'Can you even drive?' Queenie asked.

'Not legally, but I know how.'

'And where are we going to drive to?' Queenie was struggling to see the point in carrying on. '*Nowhere* is safe!'

Todd closed the trunk, the blankets bundled under his arm and the torch hanging by his side.

'We need a plan,' Queenie said, rubbing her face. 'We can't keep going like this.'

She lowered her head. The muscles in her neck burned.

'We need to stop them,' she said, filled with a sudden resolve. 'Mac-Tonic™. We need to make sure they can't make another drop of the stuff ever again.'

'I agree,' Todd said. 'But how?'

Queenie took a deep breath and sighed. Her moment of determination passed. Tears were rising behind her eyes, and when she realized that what she wanted more than anything was to be back in North Nitch with Ma and Chuckie, it made her want to cry even more.

'I don't know,' she said, looking at the ground. 'I don't know.'

Todd draped one of the blankets across Queenie's shoulders.

'We'll figure something out, OK? But maybe now isn't the best time to be making plans. We're tired and hungry and thirsty and probably traumatized by what happened today. Everything will seem better in the morning. I promise.'

'OK,' she said. 'Let's get inside.'

Todd tried the front door, but it was boarded over and refused to budge.

'Let's try round the back,' he said. 'If we force our way in through the front someone might notice and come to investigate.'

Queenie nodded. She just wanted to sleep.

At the back they found a metal door that was fastened with a thick chain and padlock, but the hinges were orange and flaky with rust. The tail of the chain hung down almost to the ground, and Todd swung it against the corroded hinges again and again. They began to disintegrate, although Queenie couldn't stand the jarring noise the links made every time they slammed against the door. She was certain the sound would carry to whoever was pursuing them through the darkening woods.

'Stand back,' Todd said, grabbing hold of the padlock, planting a foot against the wall and pulling the chain taut. He pushed hard against the wall, and after a moment the door popped away from its hinges and sent Todd sprawling.

'I may not be any good at climbing fences,' he said, getting to his feet, 'but it looks like breaking and entering might be my thing. Come on.'

Not such a liability after all, Queenie thought, and almost smiled.

Todd stepped inside and Queenie followed. They were in a storeroom, although the only thing on the shelves was a layer of dust half an inch thick. It was gloomy: there were no windows. Queenie flicked a light switch but nothing happened. Todd turned on the torch, illuminating the puffs of dust that clouded around their feet.

'I guess we expected this place to be empty,' he said. 'Let's see if there's anywhere more comfortable to sleep.'

They moved into the store itself. Thin points of light pierced through gaps around the boarded windows, and light fittings dangled precariously from the ceiling.

'This place must be really old,' Todd said.

He shone the torch at the counter, revealing an antique cash register with a rounded front. It was covered in buttons that looked like old-fashioned typewriter keys, and when Todd leaned over to press one, the drawer shot out with pelvis-shattering viciousness.

'Empty,' he said.

Queenie looked at a sign hanging above the register. Todd swept his torch beam upwards and read the cursive lettering.

'Drink Mac-Tonic™ – just 5¢ a bottle!'

'Ha,' Queenie said, without humour. 'It doesn't cost a nickel any more. More like a million.' She rubbed her head: it was still pounding. 'I'm going to find a faucet. You find somewhere we can sleep – and keep an eye on that car.'

Queenie shuffled the length of the store and passed through a doorway beyond a row of Mac-Tonic™ refrigerators. She found herself in a little office that had a small square window cut into the wall above the desk, allowing orange sunlight to flood in. There were still pieces of paper tacked to a board beside the desk, but most had fallen into a pile on the floor below, where years of damp had fused them together. There was a small safe in the corner, but it was open and empty. A green sapling grew out of the exposed filling in the seat of the desk chair.

Queenie passed through the office and reached a poky bathroom. The white tiles had developed a sickly yellow hue that was given a bit of health by the orange light spilling in from outside. She glanced into the toilet bowl and saw that it was completely dry. It didn't bode well for her next experiment. Queenie opened the faucet over the sink and waited. A shuddering noise made the faucet vibrate. A few drops of brown water dripped into the basin. Queenie sighed.

'Bad news,' she said, returning to the store. 'There's no water.'

Todd stood at the counter with his back to her. He didn't respond. He had hung the torch from one of the light fixtures, so that its beam shone down on to the broken floor. Queenie slumped on to a low shelf and drew a circle in the dust with her sneaker.

'Todd. I said, there's no water. We're probably going to die of thirst.'

'No, we're not,' he said, turning round.

Queenie took a moment to appreciate what she was seeing. Then she sprang to her feet. In each of Todd's hands was a bottle of Mac-Tonic™. They weren't the sleek, curvaceous bottles she was used to, but chunkier, homelier designs with diamond-shaped labels and swing-top stoppers.

They were both full of a dark brown liquid.

'Where did you find these?' Queenie whispered.

There was a sudden reverence for the place; the silent, dusty store took on the bearing of a sacred temple. It was as though they had found a priceless religious artefact. Which, in a way, they had.

Todd stood to one side, revealing a wooden crate on the counter where ten more bottles nestled together.

'I found them under the shelves over there.' He tipped up one of the bottles and peered through the thick glass. 'Do you think they're safe to drink? They must have been here for over fifty years.'

259

Queenie reached out and took a bottle from Todd. She handled it gently, her mouth salivating so much that she had to swallow before speaking.

'There's only one way to find out.'

She lifted the wire lever away from the bottleneck, and the top opened with a satisfying *pop*! Little bubbles rushed to the mouth of the bottle, forming a caramel foam. The sweet smell reached Queenie's nostrils and she almost wept. It was intoxicating. It was invigorating. It was Mac-Tonic™!

'Maybe start with a sip,' Todd said.

Queenie lifted the bottle to her lips and tossed her head back. She gulped as though it was a true elixir of life. Even when the foaming bubbles threatened to make her sick she kept guzzling. It would have made a fantastic commercial: she even had the label facing outwards.

Queenie drank until every last drop was gone. She stared at the bottle, glassy-eyed. And then she let out an almighty belch.

Todd raised his eyebrows. 'I'm guessing it's OK then?'

Queenie nodded, but it didn't taste as good as she remembered. Perhaps it had gone bad, after all? But still, there was something delicious about being saved by the thing she'd just sworn to destroy.

Todd opened his own bottle and took a more tentative sip. He licked his lips. 'Amazing. The sugar must have preserved it.'

'Did you find anything else?' Queenie said. The pounding in her head had disappeared, but her stomach squirmed. 'Any food?'

'Well,' Todd said, setting his bottle down on the counter. 'I found this bag of pretzels, but it doesn't sound too promising.' He gave the bag a shake. It did not sound like a bag of pretzels. He opened it up and a poured a mound of dust on to the counter.

'Hmmm,' Queenie said. 'Anything else?'

'Just this.'

He nudged a cardboard box with his foot. It contained about fifty tubes of Dr Monty's Breath Mints. Queenie stooped down and took one out. The paper they were wrapped in was thin and fragile and peeled away without any resistance. The mints were circular in shape, their edges soft and rounded. She popped one of the mints in her mouth, expecting it to break between her teeth, but instead it just crumbled.

'Not bad,' she said. 'Better than nothing. At least we'll have fresh breath – I can't remember the last time I brushed my teeth.'

She ate half the packet and then took a swig of Todd's Mac-Tonic™. She vomited frothy caramel foam almost immediately.

'Woah!' Todd said, jumping back.

The jet splattered against a boarded-up window and trickled on to the shelves below. Queenie covered her mouth with a hand.

'The Mac-Tonic™ must have gone bad,' Todd said. 'Or the mints, maybe?'

Queenie started laughing. She laughed so hard Todd began to wonder whether the Mac-Tonic™ had done something to her brain (which it had), but her hysterics were mainly due to extreme fatigue and the effect of fifteen teaspoons of sugar entering her bloodstream in one hit.

'Are you all right?' he asked.

She flapped a hand and struggled to regain her breath.

'I made myself into a soda geyser! Haven't you ever done that experiment before? I did it at elementary school, back in Kansas.'

'Oh, yeah,' he said. He looked down at the box of mints. 'Maybe we should leave a bit of time between drinking and eating, if this is all we've got. And maybe we should ration the Mac-Tonic™, too.'

'Whatever you say! You're the boss!'

Todd observed Queenie's hyperactive state with dismay. There was very little in the store to occupy her manic attention, and not much space for it either, but Queenie began to pace up and down the dusty aisles, searching for God knows what and rambling in a nonstop monologue. Todd lay down on a blanket behind the counter, but every time he fell asleep the scuffing of Queenie's footsteps or the erratic cadence of her rant would wake him.

'I'm heading out for a bit,' he called, getting up and dusting himself off.

Queenie had found a rack of tourist information leaflets, and was resuming her opportunistic reading habits from North Nitch. She gave a cheery wave but didn't look up.

'OK!'

Todd decided it was probably a good idea to take the crate of Mac-Tonic™ with him. He took the mints too. He cut through the storeroom and out the back door into the warm evening air. He made his way to the forecourt, settling into the soft driver's seat of the sedan and placing the Mac-Tonic™ and mints into the passenger footwell. Laying his head back against the headrest, he closed his eyes. Moments later, he was asleep.

He woke with a start. Someone was tapping rapidly on the window. He looked out and saw Queenie's face. It appeared even more manic in the moonlight. Wearily, warily, he opened the door.

'What is it?' he asked.

'What was the name of that observatory Cassandra mentioned?'

Todd's brain was still foggy. Queenie could have asked him who the President of the United States was and he would have needed a minute to think. So asking him about something a nutcase mentioned in passing – a couple of hungry, thirsty, sleep-deprived days ago – was like fishing in the Dead Zone.

'Labor Day . . . Camp?' he guessed.

'*Hard Labor Creek!*' Queenie said, thrusting a pamphlet at Todd.

He looked down. It was a directory of all the observatories in the South from 1954. It was printed on soft green paper.

'That's great, Queenie,' Todd said, settling back into the driver's seat. He closed his eyes. 'Really great. Why don't you come back when you've read through all the pamphlets and tell me which one is your favourite . . . in the morning.'

Queenie hit him on the side of the head with the brochure. He opened his eyes and glared at her. But then he realized that the crazed gleam in her eye was nothing to do with the sugar rush: Queenie had an idea.

'We need to go there!' she said, rushing around to the passenger side and climbing in.

'Why?' Todd asked. The contempt was gone from his voice. He sat forwards in his seat and clutched the steering wheel.

Queenie pointed up at the moon. The projection of her face shone back.

'Hard Labor Creek is where they control what gets projected up there!' she said. 'That's what Cassandra said. And if they can change it to a picture of my face, they can change it to absolutely anything.'

A momentous revelation was crashing down on Todd. He looked dazed, and it wasn't just the lack of sleep.

'Including the recipe,' he whispered.

Queenie nodded eagerly.

'But why?'

'Think about it: the only reason there's a bounty on my head is because they think I'm the only one who knows the recipe. I'm only valuable because the formula is valuable, and the formula is only valuable because it's a secret. But what if we weren't the only ones who knew the formula? What if it wasn't a secret? What if it was something everyone on the planet knew?'

The muscles in Todd's face slackened.

'I suppose that would make it worthless?' he said. 'Would that work?'

Queenie shrugged. 'It's the only way to make them stop hunting us without giving them what they want.'

'But how could we do it? The observatory must be heavily guarded.'

'It's not exactly a foolproof plan,' she said, reaching across her body and fastening her seatbelt with a *click*. 'We might have to improvise along the way.'

Todd frowned. 'What are you doing? We're not leaving now.'

'Of course we are,' Queenie said. 'The sooner we set off, the sooner this whole thing is over. It's near Atlanta. If we set off now we should be there before morning.'

Todd groaned. 'But I haven't slept properly for days. I'll fall asleep at the wheel.'

Queenie sighed and shook her head. Then she reached down into the footwell, popped open a bottle of Mac-Tonic™ and passed it across.

'Drink this,' she said.

Todd rolled his eyes, but he took the bottle and sipped.

'Sipping like a princess won't work,' Queenie said. 'Put it away!'

Todd sighed and looked at the bottle. It glinted in the moonlight. Then he lifted it to his lips and chugged it down.

Fifteen minutes later they were speeding east, the sedan's headlights illuminating the lonely stretch of road. Todd grinned at the unfolding world, wide-eyed and white-knuckled, his heart pumping sugar and caffeine at 120 beats per minute.

18

A Bunch of Psychopaths

Queenie shoved as many bottles of Mac-Tonic™ into the backpack as she could, filling the gaps around them with tubes of Dr Monty's Breath Mints.

'Supplies,' she said, catching Todd's gaze. 'In case we can't get back to the car and have to make a run for it.'

He nodded feverishly.

'Good good good,' he said. 'Almost there now.'

Five seconds later, he couldn't remember whether he'd said anything, so he repeated himself.

'Almost there now.'

And they were. The car wound its way through the richly wooded landscape of Hard Labor Creek State Park. It was still dark, and the roaming headlight beams threw long shadows deep into the woods. They passed beside a large body of water, pale moonlight rippling across its surface, before the road curved away on its gentle ascent.

Todd flicked randomly between radio stations: one minute he was singing along to a country song, the next he was listening intently to a mystic voice reading out horoscopes. He switched again to a sports station, then on to a weather report, before landing on a news programme.

'*It's day seventeen of the Great Thirst and there's still no sign of the Mac-Tonic™ formula . . .*'

'You remind me of Chuckie,' Queenie said, studying the little green booklet in the dim light. 'Always channel hopping.'

'Who's Chuckie?' Todd asked.

Queenie glanced up. She couldn't believe she hadn't mentioned Chuckie to Todd. It made her realize just how little they really knew about each other, despite how much they'd been through together.

'He's just my stupid brother,' she said, with some pride. 'What's your family like?'

Todd bent low over the steering wheel and squinted at the road. 'Oh, you know. Complicated.'

He seemed to lose his train of thought, but Queenie didn't mind so long as he kept the car on the road. She returned her attention to the brochure.

'*In other news, more and more people are joining environmental protests along the Californian coast.*

269

Demonstrations are also taking place in several major cities across the country, from New York to Houston to—'

Queenie switched the radio off and tilted the booklet to catch the moonlight.

'We're almost there. It looks like there should be a turning just a bit farther along, on the right. It might be best if we drive by to check how heavily guarded it is before doubling back.'

Todd nodded enthusiastically and then yawned like a cat.

'There it is!' Queenie said, pointing towards a dark space between the trees.

She slumped down in her seat, until she could just about see over the edge of the door. Todd didn't dare lower his speed in case it aroused suspicion, but they got a good look along the narrow lane as they passed nonetheless. Apart from a levered barrier, there didn't seem to be anything to stop them from driving straight to the observatory. Queenie glanced across at Todd and frowned. Then she looked down at the little map on the pamphlet.

'Was that definitely it?' Todd asked.

'I think so.'

He pulled on to the roadside and turned the car

around. They approached the turning and came to a stop. Queenie unfastened her seatbelt and got out.

'Be careful,' Todd said.

She glanced all around before stepping over to the barrier. The hut beside it was dark and empty. She pressed down, the metal cold against her fingertips, and the barrier rose until it stood vertically beside her. Todd drove through and stopped, allowing Queenie to lower the barrier and climb back in.

'Weird,' he said.

She nodded. 'Maybe it's a bluff. Maybe nobody comes down here because there's nothing stopping them.'

'Like the opposite of what makes people want to rob banks?' Todd said. He wasn't sure if he was making sense: his thoughts were all over the place. But it didn't matter: just then the trees on either side fell away and they found themselves in a grassy clearing, on the approach to a long building with a pale dome at either end.

'Here we are,' Queenie said. The pounding of her heart made her voice shake, and for once it was nothing to do with the lack of caffeine or sugar in her bloodstream.

'Still no sign of guards,' Todd said, pulling in near the entrance.

'No sign of anybody,' Queenie said. 'Turn the car around so we can drive off quick if things go south.'

'Good idea.'

Todd manoeuvred the car so that it was pointing back towards the gap in the trees. The faint squeal of brakes as he came to a stop was loud in the silence.

'Well,' Queenie said, taking a deep breath. 'No time like the present.'

She opened the door and stepped out. Her legs were stiff – she hadn't left the car since they set off – and the pain made her wince. She slung the backpack over her shoulder and shut the door.

'Ready?' Todd asked.

'Ready.'

They walked towards the main doors of the observatory, fully expecting to have to find a more creative way of getting into the building. But the doors swung open without resistance. They stepped inside.

The dim foyer gave way to a wide corridor that stretched the length of the building. It was deserted. The silence felt different to the one outside: man-made, somehow. A number of nondescript doors lined the wall that Queenie and Todd were facing; the wall opposite was hung with framed posters of futuristic spacecraft and distant planets. They carried slogans like: *Moon Base 2000: The Vacation of the Future!* and *Space: We'll Be There in a Jiffy*. They reminded Queenie of the covers of the science fiction novels her uncle had left behind, except these weren't advertising stories: they were real projects, long since abandoned.

Todd nudged Queenie's arm and pointed towards the door at the end of the corridor. Unlike the other doors, it had a square window cut into it. A bluish glow illuminated the room beyond. Queenie looked over her shoulder and saw an identical door at the opposite end of the corridor, but the window was black.

Queenie adjusted the strap over her shoulder, and the bottles of Mac-Tonic™ clinked slightly.

'Let's go,' she said.

They walked along the corridor as quietly as possible. They expected the doors to their right to fly open at any moment, and for someone to grab them and haul them off to an unimaginable chamber of suffering. But no one appeared.

They reached the door and peered through the window. The centre of the circular room was occupied by a huge telescope, angled towards a hole in the domed roof like an artillery gun. Beyond that, a bank of old-fashioned monitors and buttons blinked and glowed, casting everything in a frigid blue light.

'I can't see anyone,' Queenie said.

She grasped the door handle and pulled it open. They stepped inside. The only sound was a slight hum that emanated from the computers.

'There's no one here,' Todd said.

'Well, let's not hang around until someone shows up. Come on.'

They hurried around the giant telescope and stood by the terminal.

'This thing is ancient,' Queenie said, 'but that might be a good thing. Less complicated to use.'

They both peered at the rows of blue text on one of the screens. Among the jumble of code, Queenie spotted the word *WANTED*, followed a few lines later by *$10 MILLION REWARD*.

'You put your text in there,' Todd said, 'between the square brackets.'

Queenie took a deep breath.

She deleted the existing text.

She took another breath.

And then she began to enter the Mac-Tonic™ formula.

Her fingers rattled across the yellow keys, but the keyboard was more compact than she was used to, and she had to keep going back to delete her errors. She glanced over her shoulder a couple of times, but then gave up on it and focused solely on the screen. When the formula was complete she asked Todd to check through it with her.

After a minute, he nodded.

Queenie hit enter.

A box popped up requesting, in blocky text, to confirm the changes. Queenie's index finger punched the key again. Another box popped up, containing one word: *INITIATE*.

Two square buttons at opposite ends of the console began to flash between red and white. They'd been placed far apart to ensure that no one could tamper with the Lunar Projection System on their own. It was the same mechanism they used to prevent rogue nuclear missile launches.

Queenie and Todd rushed to either end of the terminal.

'Are you ready?' she asked.

Todd nodded. 'Ready.'

'Together, on three. One. Two. *Three*.'

They pushed the buttons simultaneously.

The bank of monitors died; the screens went black. A hidden mechanism whirred for a few seconds before clunking to a stop. The room was dark; the only illumination came from the moonlight flooding in through the hole in the roof.

Behind them, someone clapped with exaggerated slowness. They spun around. Standing beside the telescope, his hands clasped in front of his chest, was Dwight Eagleman.

'Bravo,' he said. 'That really was quite a show.'

Queenie's heart was an elevator car in free fall. Something seemed to be blocking her windpipe. She felt beyond weak.

'What are you doing here?' she said.

Dwight Eagleman smiled a smile he'd been practising his whole life. It was a real winner.

'I'm here to tell you that it's all over, Miss de la Cruz. You did an excellent job. Truly excellent. I really couldn't have asked for more. You were wonderful.'

Queenie frowned. 'What do you mean?'

Dwight Eagleman's smile widened.

'Miss de la Cruz, you are at the centre of the most audacious, elaborate marketing campaign in the history of the world. You are the subject of a global manhunt. There is, as I'm sure you're aware, a ten-million-dollar bounty on your head. Your face is on the moon. The Mac-Tonic™ Corporation has never had so much publicity, nor so many thirsty customers. When Mac-Tonic™ returns to the shelves, we will sell an unprecedented amount. And it's all because of you.'

'I don't understand,' Queenie said. 'It doesn't make sense . . .'

Dwight Eagleman took a step forwards. Out of the corner of her eye, Queenie saw Todd edge closer to her.

'I assure you that it does,' Dwight Eagleman said. 'Everything that has happened to you since you found that recipe has been controlled by me. You are not here by accident. You are here because I led you here.'

Queenie needed to press pause on everything. Questions tripped over each other in her mouth, but one tumbled out ahead of the rest.

'Why me? How did you know that I would find the recipe?'

Dwight Eagleman took another step forwards, moving out of the moonlight and into shadow.

'That was an . . . unanticipated development. The formula was never supposed to wash up: it was supposed to be lost when those planes collided. I'd already destroyed the original copy kept in the company vault, clearing the way for it to be miraculously rediscovered – by me – when demand for Mac-Tonic™ reached critical levels. But everything worked out so much better this way. And I still get to take all the credit.'

Queenie was in shock. She couldn't speak.

'Miss de la Cruz, surely you've worked out by now that we control everything.' He swept a hand around the shadowy observatory. 'How did you come to hear about this place, for example?'

Queenie swallowed. 'A woman called Cassandra told us.'

Dwight Eagleman's face broke into a fond, fatherly expression. 'And how is Cassandra? Is she still wearing those little foil hats? Does she still import her drinking water from Montana?'

Queenie was crestfallen. She'd based almost everything on the tall tales of a stooge.

'Do you really think a woman as paranoid as Cassandra could resist being part of a conspiracy like this? A young girl on the run from a big, bad corporation? I knew she'd help you, because I know how people think. Especially people like her. People like you.'

Queenie was desperate to find some hole in the story, some inconsistency, but fragments were already beginning to slot into place: the miraculous getaways; the unlikely alliances; the car on the forecourt with a full tank of gas. She thought back to Area 51 – the ease of their escape, the searchlight guiding the way – and felt like a fool.

And then she remembered something Cassandra said, something she had been unwilling to believe at the time: *If you escaped, it must be because they wanted you to escape.*

'It hasn't been easy,' Dwight Eagleman said, edging ever closer, 'plotting your course with an invisible hand, casting the net wide while making sure there were gaps just big enough for you to slip through.'

'We could have been killed,' Queenie mumbled. 'The black helicopters—'

'Were sent to protect you. I admit there were a couple of close calls along the way, but you pulled through. Besides, I never needed you for the formula. I'd never leave that to chance.'

Queenie felt sick. 'You mean you had a copy of the recipe all along?' She pointed at the dead terminal behind her. 'This wasn't some kind of trap to recover it?'

Dwight Eagleman took another step forwards. 'I don't have a copy of the Mac-Tonic™ formula, but Delixir™ Enterprises does.'

'What?' Todd asked. It was more of a croak. It was the first thing he'd said since Dwight Eagleman's arrival.

'You know what they say: keep your friends close and your enemies closer. It may seem as though we hate each other, but we are simply two sides of the same coin. One could not exist without the other. There must be balance.'

Dwight Eagleman took a final step forwards. He was close enough to reach out and lay a reassuring hand on Queenie's shoulder, but he did not.

'The reason why Delixir™ has a copy of the Mac-Tonic™ formula is because Mac-Tonic™ and Delixir™ are exactly the same thing.'

Queenie was dizzy. She didn't know what or who to believe. The words were so paradoxical, so blasphemous, so absurd that the walls of the observatory should have fallen away to reveal a landscape of stark, blinding whiteness, stretching away to infinity.

Todd groaned at the other end of the console, and Queenie looked over. He had his head in his hands. Queenie wished he wasn't standing so far away.

'Don't look to him for answers,' Dwight Eagleman

said. 'He's disappointed you almost as much as he's disappointed me.'

Todd swallowed hard and glared at Dwight Eagleman, who just smiled that winning smile.

'Did he ever tell you the nickname they gave him on his very first day at The Mac-Tonic™ Corporation?'

Queenie felt as though she was being gored. There was something unnatural lodged in her chest.

'No? Well, I suppose to tell you that would have meant explaining a lot of inconvenient facts. They called him the Kennedy Kid.'

'Dad,' Todd said. There was real hurt in the word.

Dwight Eagleman raised a hand. 'No.'

Queenie felt as though whatever had been lodged in her chest had just been yanked out.

'He's your *father*?' she asked.

Todd nodded, but he couldn't bring himself to meet her wounded gaze.

'And you were working for Mac-Tonic™ all along?' It was an effort just to talk.

Todd shook his head, defeated.

'Not quite,' Dwight Eagleman said. 'Not intentionally, anyway. He's been working for Delixir™.'

'What?' Queenie asked. Suddenly she had enough breath to shout, and she didn't waste it. 'Why?'

'You know what they're like,' Todd spat, jabbing a finger towards his father. 'You know all about the terrible things they've done. And he expected me to follow in his footsteps! You should hear them in their board meetings. It's like listening to a bunch of psychopaths!'

'It's just business,' Dwight Eagleman said mildly.

'I didn't want anything to do with Mac-Tonic™ – I wanted to ruin it – and so I went to Delixir™ to see what I could do. They sent me straight to Area 51. I'd only been there an hour or so when they brought you in.'

Queenie didn't know how to feel: she switched from anger to pity to incomprehension three times a second. She remembered Todd's tale of torture – the horror and sympathy it had inspired in her – and felt utterly foolish.

'Why didn't you tell me the truth?' she asked.

'I wanted to but . . . I didn't want you to think I was one of *them*. I'm on your side, I promise. They asked me to keep you away from Mac-Tonic™ until the company folded, so that Delixir™ could take over.' Todd shook his head. 'I didn't realize back then they were in it together. That it was all just one big marketing stunt.'

His chest heaved up and down. He fixed his father with a hard stare. 'People died! Don't you care?'

Dwight Eagleman regarded his son coolly. 'There is no reward without risk. No war has ever been won without bloodshed. Everything that was done was done for the greater good of The Mac-Tonic™ Corporation.'

And with that, Dwight Eagleman leaned towards the bank of monitors, lifted a clear plastic cover and pressed the little red button cowering beneath. The screens flickered to life, a great whirring began and the moonlight pouring through the retractable panel in the roof shifted from white to red; the moon, once again, resembled the cap of a Mac-Tonic™ bottle. It was a beacon that would bring hope to a parched world.

The Great Thirst was over.

Queenie rushed to Todd, grabbed his hand and ran towards the exit. Dwight Eagleman didn't move from the console. They were halfway across the room when their way out was blocked by a group of men wearing black suits and dark shades. They skidded to a halt beside the base of the great telescope.

'I'm afraid I can't let you leave,' Dwight Eagleman said, turning to face them.

Queenie glared at him.

'What are you going to do to us?' she asked.

'I'm sure no one would believe you if you were to share what I've told you tonight, but I just can't take the risk. You both know too much. Todd will be returning to Area 51 – for real this time, and for ever. And you, Queenie . . .' He looked at her like a man forced to sell his favourite car. 'You've caused a lot of trouble. People are upset. They want justice. And what kind of man would I be to deny them?'

His eyes lingered on Queenie's anguished face before sliding towards the men at the door. They began their approach.

'Wait!' Todd said.

Dwight Eagleman raised a finger. Backlit by the monitors, he looked like a saint. The men stopped.

'Why don't we have one last drink?' Todd said, his voice bitter. 'For old times' sake.'

He unzipped the backpack hanging from Queenie's shoulder and withdrew a bottle of Mac-Tonic™. The men in suits reached inside their jackets, but Dwight Eagleman kept that righteous finger raised. Todd tossed the bottle to his father, who caught it in one hand. It was the first time he'd ever played catch with his son. He inspected the old bottle with great affection.

'Where did you find this?' he asked.

'Does it matter?'

Todd withdrew another bottle and popped the swing-top open. Caramel foam fizzed to the top. He raised it in a toast.

'To Mac-Tonic™,' he said.

Dwight Eagleman popped the cap and raised his own bottle. 'To Mac-Tonic™.'

They both drank.

And then, in one swift movement, Todd dropped a whole roll of Dr Monty's Breath Mints into the fizzing liquid, stoppered the bottle and flung it at the waiting goons. It shattered at their feet, detonating like a grenade, throwing glass shrapnel across the room.

'Come on!' Todd shouted, scrambling up the shaft of the telescope, scurrying in a half crouch towards the gap in the dome. Queenie flung her backpack aside and followed close behind. Todd reached the lens and leaped for the opening. He landed with one foot on the rim, steadied himself with a hand and turned back to reach for Queenie.

She took the last few steps at a run and jumped towards Todd. Their fingers were almost touching when a hand closed around her ankle. It belonged to Dwight

Eagleman, and his grip was like a vice. Queenie landed hard on her chest and slid off the side of the telescope.

'Queenie!' Todd shouted, certain the fall would kill her.

But one of the goons caught her, and within seconds they had her pinned to the floor.

'Run!' she shouted.

There was nothing Todd could do. He slid down the outside of the roof, jumped to the ground and ran to the car. He fumbled the key into the ignition and finally got it to turn. Two goons emerged from the building just in time to see him accelerate along the track between the trees. He crashed through the barrier, swerved on to the road and raced away.

To Eat a Beating Heart

Queenie was captured in the early hours of Saturday morning; her trial began on Monday.

With one swipe of his magisterial hand, Alexander Greenberg had cleared the court's schedule, adjourning indefinitely whatever two-bit proceeding had been underway – a serial killer or terrorist plotter or something else equally trifling. He made a system clogged with bureaucracy and incompetence and hypocrisy flow like a wide river of retribution. He knew which palms to grease and how well to grease them and made sure that they were as slick as an oil spill by Monday morning.

To all intents and purposes, Queenie's was to be a show trial. Nobody really questioned her guilt. If Mac-Tonic™ said it was so, it must be so. But unfortunately this was a democracy, and so some semblance of due process was required to make the ruling appear righteous, instead of vengeful. It was of paramount importance that Queenie de la Cruz did not become a martyr the moment they pumped her full of potassium chloride. That would be bad for business.

Due to the phenomenal publicity associated with the case, it was deemed impossible to find an impartial jury – Queenie's face had been projected on to the moon, after all – so the case went to a bench trial. Judge Walter Waldroop was appointed to oversee proceedings, which was great news for Alexander Greenberg as the judge had ruled favourably in two historic Mac-Tonic™ cases, and was also a known guzzler of the sweet stuff. According to some, he got through three gallons of it a week. If anybody in California was going to see Queenie de la Cruz punished to the full extent of the law, it was Judge Walter Waldroop.

'I can't wait!' Randy van de Velde said, rubbing his hands. 'It's gonna be a turkey shoot, Al, I just know it!'

Alexander Greenberg shook his head. They were standing in one of the courthouse conference rooms, waiting for the trial to begin.

'You're not coming into the courtroom, Randy.'

Randy van de Velde looked appalled. 'Whaddya mean? I flew in from New York specially. I even picked up a new suit!'

Alexander Greenberg was neatly layering papers in his briefcase. He snapped it shut.

'Randy, I know how much this case means to you. But trust me, you'll lose your cool the moment you see that little girl.' He placed a hand on Randy's shoulder, to stop him from losing his cool now. 'It means a lot that you came – it really does – but this is something I have to do alone. There's a reason Dwight and the others didn't come: it won't look good if there's a pack of us and just one of her. It'll send out the wrong impression. So why don't you stay in here and watch it on TV?'

Randy van de Velde nodded grimly. He felt like an all-star being left on the bench for the big game. Alexander Greenberg gave him a brave smile, reached down for the remote and turned on the TV attached to the wall. Randy van de Velde fell into a chair and turned the volume up.

On the screen, Bruce Dillinger smiled manically, like a ventriloquist's doll. The Death-o-Meter was gone, and the scrolling banner at the bottom of the screen declared:

--- MAC-TONIC™ BACK IN PRODUCTION ---
FIRST BATCH TO HIT SHELVES BY THE END OF
THE WEEK --- PUBLIC HOLIDAY DECLARED AUG 1 ---

'Mac-Tonic™ share prices hit an all-time high when markets opened this morning,' Bruce Dillinger announced, 'and they're expected to keep on climbing with the prosecution of Queenie de la Cruz.'

'Amen!' Randy van de Velde yelled.

'We're joined now by our expert in all things legal, Craig Fitzwilliam. Craig, you worked for fifteen years as a janitor in the very courthouse where this trial is taking place – how do you think things are going to play out today?'

'Well, she's guilty all right.'

There was a three-second pause that, on live TV, opened like a chasm of awkwardness.

'Do you want to add anything else?' Bruce Dillinger asked.

Craig licked his lips. 'This just goes to show what happens when you let foreigners into our country. I think the whole case is a waste of government dollars. They should just take her to the roof and throw her off. It's plenty high enough, trust me – I had to clean every floor.'

Bruce turned back to the camera. 'Thanks for that insight, Craig. We'll come back to you when the verdict's in. But now we can go live to our news chopper, which is following Queenie de la Cruz's car on its way to the courthouse.'

A motorcade made its way along the cleared streets: a black SUV surrounded by squad cars and motorbikes. Thousands of people had gathered on the sidewalks, hoping to catch a glimpse of the nation's most notorious villain. It was like watching the world's slowest car chase. The network producer put in a prayer for something dramatic to happen, but the big guy upstairs must have been busy, because the motorcade progressed without incident.

Alexander Greenberg could hear chanting from below, and the news helicopters circling above. He drifted over to the window just as the black SUV pulled up outside the courthouse. A man got out, walked around the rear of the car and opened the back door.

Queenie de la Cruz stepped down from the vehicle.

Even at ground level, Queenie looked too small to be the centre of such a media frenzy. She shuffled forwards, between crowds that had been parted like a biblical sea. The people shouted and held up banners, but she couldn't tell what they were saying, and the posters may as well have been written in Spanish for all the sense she could make of them. She suddenly felt very alone. She had no idea whether Ma and Chuckie would be at the hearing, but she hoped they would.

Suddenly, there was a scream that skewered her through the noise, and it was followed by three shots. *Pop! Pop! Pop!* Queenie didn't see the muzzle flash – didn't even have time to flinch. The security detail closed in tight around her and bustled her towards the courthouse. She had no idea if she'd been hit. She drew great gulping breaths but couldn't get enough air into her lungs. She couldn't feel anything: her body was numb, a tingling mass that didn't seem to belong to her any more.

They were almost at the courthouse. She glanced back, looking for the trail of blood – her blood, great gouts of it splattered on the sidewalk – but couldn't see any. Firm hands pressed against her back and shoulders. *Are they staunching the flow? Saving me for the lethal injection?*

Just before she was bustled through the revolving doors and into the cool quiet of the lobby, Queenie caught sight of a scuffle. It was the cops, wrestling a man to the ground. She hadn't expected to recognize her assailant, but she did. It's not easy to forget someone's face after they've offered you three million dollars and a lifetime's supply of Mac-Tonic™. It was Randy van de Velde.

Once inside the relative safety of the foyer, one of the security agents checked Queenie over for gunshot wounds. There were none. She was just in shock. A glass of water and a sit down and she'd be right as rain. Randy van de Velde's shots had missed her by mere inches, zipping out into the world like little nuggets of blind cruelty, to do what bullets are designed to do.

Peering down from his vantage point in the conference room, Alexander Greenberg was furious. Randy van de Velde's assassination attempt had almost stolen his glory. The girl's fate was his to seal, and his alone.

He checked his watch, snatched up his briefcase and strode from the room.

Queenie sat alone in the courtroom. The public defender appointed to her had had a change of heart – he was taking the innumerable death threats he'd received seriously – and abandoned Queenie to face the American justice system alone. So help her God.

Queenie had expected there to be a jury: twelve strangers who would spend hours or days or weeks being subtly plied by a skilled manipulator until they saw things the same way as him. Queenie had tried to imagine what each of the jurors might look like: whether any of them would be on her side, whether any of them would be friendly. But there was no jury. Queenie had not understood what a bench trial was, and she'd been too afraid to ask. Her representative had been very nervous around her: he hated socializing with death rowers. He had been convinced that life imprisonment without parole would be a great victory. He sold it to Queenie like a travel agent selling two weeks in the Caribbean.

In a way, even though it meant she was alone, Queenie was glad that he had abandoned her. She glanced behind, searching the audience for Ma and Chuckie – and there they were! Queenie had never seen her mother look so smart, and even Chuckie had been persuaded to wear a suit and tie. She had an almost irresistible desire to call out, to wave, but she realized just in time how it would look to the rest of the courtroom. Instead, she turned back to the front, before anybody had chance to see her eyes. But the cameras caught it all. Hundreds of millions of people saw the tears that gathered and glistened and threatened to fall. There was nothing else on TV, after all.

A clerk stood up at the front. The courtroom rose as Judge Waldroop's arrival was announced. Queenie's legs shook and nearly buckled. She steadied herself by placing slick fingertips on the table before her.

Judge Walter Waldroop swept into the room in fluttering black robes. Alexander Greenberg almost did a double take. He barely recognized him, even though they'd played many rounds of golf together over the years. In the absence of Mac-Tonic™, Judge Waldroop had lost twenty pounds in three weeks. He was sleeping like a baby. He had time for his wife and kids. He was a new man. Gone was the laborious waddle, the heavy collapse into his seat, the lethargic shuffle of documents; Judge Waldroop positively sprang to the bench. He looked out at the courtroom with a smile of wonderment, adjusted his thin-framed glasses as though he couldn't believe his eyes, and took his place with elegance and poise.

If Alexander Greenberg was rattled by the transformation, he didn't show it. In fact, as he launched into his opening statement, it was hard not to be impressed by his eloquence, his passion, his restraint. He didn't raise his voice, or even a righteous finger. He was smooth and measured and – it seemed – entirely reasonable. It was like releasing a giant fish – dulled by long years of captivity in an aquarium tank – into the vastness of the ocean. *This* was where he truly belonged. He could survive out there, of course, in the everyday world, and people would stare at him and be convinced that they were viewing the true animal. But it was *here*, in the halls of justice and reason and retribution, that he was able to dart and dive and *hunt*. No more scoops of chum for him! It was time to sink his teeth. It was time to eat a beating heart.

Like all good predators, he was on to his victim long before she detected his presence. For even Queenie felt herself being taken in, transported by his monologue, scowling inwardly at the dastardly subject of his speech. It was, at times, as though he wasn't even speaking. It felt as though his hand was reaching inside the minds of his listeners, planting new ideas and quietly snuffing out any traces of doubt. The manipulation, as true manipulation has to be, was subtle.

But Queenie was beginning to detect the duplicity of his words. She realized, with a jolt, that she was the one being described. The way Alexander Greenberg outlined the circumstances leading to Queenie's arrest made it seem as though she had had a clear choice at every turn, and yet she had chosen a path of criminality and destruction. Abduction became absconding, Mac-Tonic™ had launched a search and not a manhunt, and Queenie's flight from a murderous mob became resisting the will of the people. Alexander Greenberg omitted crucial information: the terrifying tactics that had been used to pursue her, the fact that Dwight Eagleman's son had abetted her, and, most crucially of all, that Dwight Eagleman had masterminded the whole episode. *Does he even know that part?* They were omissions that should have collapsed the whole case, but it remained standing by virtue of Alexander Greenberg's magical rhetoric.

And then it was time for Queenie to take the stand.

Her chair gave a little squeak as she pushed it back and stood up. She made her way slowly, tentatively, to the box. She felt as though gravity had become a variable force: one step felt dizzyingly easy, the next was clumsy and laboured. She wondered what her gait looked like to the people watching – the millions of people watching – and quickly thought of something else. She focused on the American flag hanging limply on its pole behind Judge Walter Waldroop. It was so still she couldn't be sure if it was a real flag or a sculpture.

She reached the witness box and turned to face the courtroom. A Bible was offered up, and she placed a hand upon it. She raised her other hand in a Girl Scout salute.

'You do solemnly state that the testimony you may give in the case now pending before this court shall be the truth, the whole truth and nothing but the truth, so help you God?'

Conversations with her representative crowded Queenie's thoughts: his advice had swung from denying everything and hoping for some kind of pardon, to remembering who they were up against and imploring Queenie to just plead guilty to everything, no matter what. But the oath had given her a novel idea: she resolved to tell the truth. Not the whole truth, of course; this wasn't the place to disclose all the atrocities that had been committed in the name of *Mac-Tonic*™ – no one was ready for that kind of revelation. But the truth, nonetheless.

She looked up at Judge Waldroop and thought she saw some kindness, some understanding, in his eyes. Everything – her life, her death – would be decided by this one man. It was a terrifying thought.

Queenie nodded. 'I do.'

She lifted her hand away from the Bible and it was taken away. Her fingers left dark marks on the cover.

'Miss de la Cruz,' Alexander Greenberg said, with a smile. 'Please could you explain, in your own words, how you came into possession of the Mac-Tonic™ formula?'

Queenie gazed around the courtroom, trying to ignore the cameras, and then glanced up at Judge Waldroop. He gave a slow nod and sat forwards in his chair.

'It washed up,' Queenie said.

The clerk immediately sprang forwards and angled the microphone closer to Queenie's mouth. He retreated without a smile.

Alexander Greenberg looked down at his notes, even though he had no need to consult them. It was simply a gesture to make Queenie more comfortable, so that she didn't feel under scrutiny, so that she would open up and incriminate herself with her own testimony. Years of experience had taught him that the best prosecutor is often the defendant.

'Could you provide a little more information, Miss de la Cruz?'

She cleared her throat. 'It washed up in a bottle, on the beach outside my home in North Nitch, California.'

Queenie had never thought of the ramshackle house as her home, but the word suddenly felt natural and bittersweet on her tongue. She knew that she would probably never see it again.

'Could you describe the appearance of the formula, and the bottle it washed up in?'

'The formula was written on the back of a Mac-Tonic™ label and rolled up inside a Mac-Tonic™ bottle.'

'Was there a label on the bottle?'

'No. They used the label from the bottle to write the message.'

'In which case, how could you be certain that it was a Mac-Tonic™ bottle, and not the bottle of a rival brand?'

Queenie shot Alexander Greenberg a look that she normally reserved for Chuckie's most idiotic comments. Chuckie recognized it at once, and swelled with pride.

'Because of the shape. Everybody knows the shape of a Mac-Tonic™ bottle. I've drunk from hundreds – thousands – of them over the years. Besides, Mac-Tonic™ bottles are always washing up on the shore. You can't move for them.'

Alexander Greenberg allowed himself a small smile. *Self-incriminating and a marketer's dream.* Maybe the data about the Great Pacific Garbage Patch had been wrong. Maybe their trash did constitute at least fifty-one per cent.

'And what did you do when you discovered the recipe?'

'I told my family.' Queenie swallowed. She couldn't bring herself to look at them.

Alexander Greenberg nodded. 'Your Honour, what we're about to hear is a recording of that conversation.' He nodded to the clerk.

The courtroom listened to the conversation Queenie had had with Chuckie and Ma through her bedroom door. The first part was partially obscured by the intermittent, inane jingling of a never-ending phone game, but the conversation was clear enough. When it came to an end, Judge Waldroop raised his eyebrows. Alexander Greenberg seemed satisfied. He turned back to Queenie.

'Could you tell the court what happened next, Miss de la Cruz?'

'Three men from Mac-Tonic™, including you, turned up at the house and offered my family money.'

Alexander Greenberg paused. It was deliberate. Everything with him was deliberate.

'How much money were you offered, Miss de la Cruz?'

Queenie leaned in close to the microphone. 'Three million dollars.'

There was a gasp from the audience. Clothes rustled and benches creaked. A quick look from Judge Waldroop stilled them. Alexander Greenberg shook his head sadly, as though he really regretted Queenie's predicament.

'Thank you, Miss de la Cruz, that will be all.'

Queenie couldn't believe that her time on the stand was over. She'd expected to be interrogated for hours, asked the same questions again and again while Alexander Greenberg pecked at the smallest inconsistencies in her account until the whole thing was in tatters.

As she stepped down and returned to her hard chair she realized why Alexander Greenberg had asked her so little: he didn't want her to give her version of events. She would have described the abduction, the true purpose of Area 51, the fear she had felt, the terrible things she had learned, the various attempts that had been made on her young life. All of it was relevant to the case, but none of it was relevant to Alexander Greenberg's case.

Queenie regretted leaving the stand so abruptly, and longed to be given another chance to speak. She even stood up, but was quickly forced back into her seat by a stern glance from the judge. Alexander Greenberg was talking again.

'When that Mac-Tonic™ bottle washed up on the shores of our great country, in this fine state of California, Miss de la Cruz had a choice. She could either hand over the formula it contained to its rightful owner, The Mac-Tonic™ Corporation, for a handsome reward, or she could choose to flee, depriving the world of its favourite beverage.

'As we now know, Miss de la Cruz opted to take the latter path. She could have surrendered herself to the authorities at any time, but instead she chose the life of a fugitive. She led us on a merry chase, costing the taxpayer millions of dollars in the process. Thousands of people lost their lives because of her recklessness, and the blood of those people is on her hands.

'She was apprehended at Hard Labor Creek Observatory, Georgia, in the nick of time. Her wicked intention had been to project the sacred formula on to the moon for all to see – no matter their nationality or ideology or politics. She planned to disclose one of our nation's most fiercely guarded secrets indiscriminately. Naturally, this would have included the enemies of the United States of America. If Miss de la Cruz had succeeded, by now there would be imitation Mac-Tonic™ being produced in places like Russia, China and *Mexico*.'

He looked hard at Queenie, and his eyes revealed that there would be no mercy.

'Miss de la Cruz's decision to share the Mac-Tonic™ recipe was not only unconscionable, it was also un-American. We have – and I do not use this word lightly – a *traitor* in our midst. And there is only one punishment befitting an act of high treason.'

He didn't say the word – he was too wise to call for her execution outright – but he did pause, and the silence of that pause was like a death itself. It gave everyone an opportunity to imagine Queenie's fate for themselves. It became their idea, too.

Alexander Greenberg closed the folder of papers on his table with a casual gesture. It was all symbolic, all calculated. The message was clear: there is nothing left to consider, this case is now closed. He straightened his back, clasped his hands together and addressed Judge Walter Waldroop.

'Your Honour, I ask that this court finds Queenie de la Cruz guilty of the crime of treason, and request that she is prohibited – permanently – from attempting to commit such a heinous offence against the people of this great country ever again.'

He bowed his head slightly and returned to his seat. There was nothing to be heard but the faint rustle of paper and the occasional creak as someone shifted in their seat. Finally, Judge Waldroop seemed to stir from his reverie and turned to regard Queenie.

'Miss de la Cruz, would you like to say anything before we proceed to judgement?'

Queenie found herself nodding and climbing shakily to her feet before she had any idea of what she might say. But she knew she had to speak: this was her last chance. She took a breath to compose herself, but it juddered on the way in and juddered on the way out, and only served to remind her of how terrified she was.

'Thank you, Your Honour.' Queenie's voice wobbled. She cleared her throat. She carried on. 'I think Mr Greenberg must be a very good lawyer. He talks so well that even I'm wondering if maybe I am guilty of the things he says I am. But I'm not. There's a whole other side to this story that he didn't even mention. He didn't say anything about the fact I've been kidnapped – twice – in the past week, or that I've been held at gunpoint, or that Mac-Tonic™ turned everyone against me, or that my only friend since this whole thing began was Todd Eagleman – Dwight Eagleman's son – who was so appalled by what Mac-Tonic™ stands for that he turned against his own father.'

Queenie gulped another lungful of air. Her heart pounded so hard it made her vision shake. She had no idea whether she was saying the right things, but she had to keep going.

'If any one person clung to power like Mac-Tonic™ does, we'd call them a tyrant, and we'd kick them out. We're not supposed to have kings in this country. It's *them*' – she pointed a finger at Alexander Greenberg – 'who are un-American. It's them who are traitors.'

She wanted to say more – to repeat the fabulous accusations she'd heard outside Area 51 – but she had no evidence. They would be swept aside, laughed at, used as proof of Queenie's dangerous instability.

'Mac-Tonic™ likes to pretend it's an all-American company. It wants you to believe it stands for freedom and choice and good times. But how free have people felt without it, these past few weeks? People are slaves to it!

Slaves to a bottle of fizzy sugar-water! And how much choice do we really have? I've travelled thousands of miles this past week, and all I've seen is Delixir™ and Mac-Tonic™ on every billboard. Call that a choice? They're the same thing!'

There was a collective gasp from the audience behind her. It was hard to imagine anyone saying such a thing, especially after swearing on the Holy Bible.

'It's true!' Queenie said, glancing around at the shocked faces. 'If you don't believe me, drink it blindfolded and try to work out which one you're tasting. And as for good times, do you think our towns and cities are better places for the Mac-Tonic™ bottles littering the streets? Do you think people like wading through trash to take a walk in the park, or to swim in the ocean? And what about the creatures that *live* in those oceans? Do you think they like sharing their home with a bunch of plastic bottles?'

Queenie had no idea how she'd ended up campaigning to save the dolphins. Wasn't she supposed to be trying to save herself? Maybe they were the same thing.

And then she recalled something wise someone had said what felt like a lifetime ago. Something that had made her stop and think and act. Something that had led her to this very moment.

'It's your world too,' she said.

Her shoulders slumped. She shook her head. There were tears in her eyes, and they trickled into her voice as well.

'Whatever,' she said. 'I guess everyone's made up their minds already. Just know that there's no way in hell my last meal is going to include Mac-Tonic™.'

Of all the things Queenie had said, this last comment was the only one to draw a reaction from Alexander Greenberg. It was galling: a personal insult. Queenie would have the last laugh, even on her way to the execution chamber. It spoiled his victory, and his handsome face puckered into an ugly scowl.

Queenie looked up at Judge Waldroop in something of a daze.

'That's all I've got to say, Your Honour.'

She slumped into her chair. Judge Waldroop arched his eyebrows. He'd heard some closing statements in his time, but none quite like Queenie's. He looked down at the paperwork spread neatly before him and frowned.

'I was going to call for a recess at this juncture, but I can see little point in that.' He looked up and regarded the court. 'I am ready to deliver my judgement.'

Queen's insides shrivelled away. Her torso felt hollow and raw, as though someone had scraped it out with a shovel. There was to be no recess. Judge Waldroop wasn't even going to consider the case. Queenie saw now that his mind had been made up from the start.

'It appears to me that your entire case, Mr Greenberg, is built on the contention that the bottle that washed up in North Nitch, California, and the contents therein – namely the Mac-Tonic™ formula – belong to The Mac-Tonic™ Corporation. During her cross-examination the defendant, Miss de la Cruz, confirmed under oath that this was indeed the case. I therefore have no choice but to uphold the assertion made by Mr Greenberg. The bottle and its contents remain the legal property of The Mac-Tonic™ Corporation unless proof of purchase can be provided by a third party.' His eyes slid from Alexander Greenberg to Queenie. 'No such receipt has been forthcoming from the defence, namely because the defence possesses no such document.'

Queenie sank lower in her chair. Beneath his table, Alexander Greenberg clenched his hand into a victorious fist, but his face remained impassive. He wasn't about to get thrown out of court for whooping and fist pumping.

'It is therefore the ruling of this court that the formula shall be returned to its rightful owner, The Mac-Tonic™ Corporation. As Miss de la Cruz has already fulfilled this order, albeit by slightly unconventional means, no further action is required on the part of Miss de la Cruz.'

She didn't understand. *Is that it? Is it over?* Judge Waldroop offered her a small, pitying smile before turning his attention to Alexander Greenberg. He removed his glasses. It was a significant gesture, like rolling up one's sleeves.

'Mr Greenberg, I have found your conduct today to be presumptuous, arrogant and downright vindictive. You have stood before this court, as a representative of The Mac-Tonic™ Corporation, and called for the execution of a minor. You ought to be ashamed of yourself.'

It was all very well, handing out recommendations for how Alexander Greenberg *should* be feeling, but unfortunately he was not the kind of person to feel shame. Or any other redemptive emotion, for that matter. Beneath the table, his fist began to unfurl.

'The defendant is cleared of the charge of treason. No further action will be taken against her.'

Queenie struggled to sit up straight. She was convinced that she had fallen asleep and was dreaming.

Or that her veins were already full of potassium chloride, and her brain was misfiring and misremembering as death soaked through her. But Judge Waldroop was not done yet.

'However, Miss de la Cruz's closing statement has brought another crime to the court's attention: The Mac-Tonic™ Corporation's abuse of this planet. I'll admit I'm not sure of this court's jurisdiction on the matter, but I *can* rule on one factor both parties agree upon: the Mac-Tonic™ bottle that washed up near the de la Cruz residence is the property of The Mac-Tonic™ Corporation. It therefore follows that the trillions of other Mac-Tonic™ bottles polluting our oceans *also* belong to The Mac-Tonic™ Corporation.'

Alexander Greenberg could see where this was going, and he was horrified. He was like a child at a fairground who had wanted bumper cars but got the ghost train instead, and now his cart was heading for the rickety doors and swirling smoke and impenetrable darkness; the glowing eyes and tickly cobwebs and grisly waxworks; the howling and shrieking and cackling laughter. He began to sweat. He wanted out.

'Therefore, this court also rules that The Mac-Tonic™ Corporation is responsible for *all* of its bottles, and orders the company to foot the bill for a global clean-up operation.'

Alexander Greenberg stood up. 'Your Honour, this is unacceptable—'

'Please sit down and remain silent, Mr Greenberg.'

'But the ruling is unjust! There's absolutely no evidence to confirm the bottle that washed up was a Mac-Tonic™ bottle – all we have is the statement of a little girl.'

He flung an accusatory hand in Queenie's direction. Judge Waldroop's frown deepened.

'Mr Greenberg, you were happy to use her testimony for your own purposes a few moments ago. I'm afraid you can't pick and choose the evidence that suits you: that's not how justice works.'

'It is for us!'

There was much rustling and whispering from the back of the court. Police officers and court officials began to make their way to the front.

'Mr Greenberg, if you do not calm yourself I will have you forcibly removed from my courtroom.'

'Your courtroom? *Your* courtroom! This is *my* courtroom, Walt, and you know it! This is the last time you'll ever put on that robe! They won't even let you clean the toilets when I'm done with you!'

Judge Waldroop nodded to the waiting officers, and they closed in around Alexander Greenberg. He fought and writhed and tried to break free from the hands that held him.

'I'll take this to the Supreme Court, you hear me? I'll appeal this all the way! The President will hear about this! Get your hands off me, you pigs!'

Everyone watched Alexander Greenberg disappear through the courtroom doors. His voice bounced off the corridor walls, adding to its hysteria, until the doors eased shut and there was order once more.

Judge Waldroop turned to Queenie with a weary expression. 'Miss de la Cruz,' he said simply, 'you are free to go.'

Queenie's heart soared. She jumped to her feet, desperate to reach Ma and Chuckie, but a swarm of reporters closed in around her. Their competing voices clashed into nonsense, their bristling equipment poked and prodded her. She forced her way to the door, and with the help of two court officials she made the corridor. A gap opened between two journalists as they spilled into the larger space, and Queenie ran. Feet thudded along the corridor behind her. The reporters called her name and asked her questions and demanded a statement, but Queenie kept running.

She could hear the crowd outside now, could see the reflections of their colourful posters on the marble walls of the lobby. The thought of facing the mob made her hesitate – one of them had tried to assassinate her, after all – but then she looked back at the flood of reporters and knew she had to take her chances. She barged through the revolving doors, bracing herself for the barrage of bullets and abuse, and came to an abrupt halt.

A deafening cheer hit her like a wall. The people were smiling, clapping, chanting her name. She had been too preoccupied to notice on the way in, but now she saw that their banners and posters were covered in slogans of support, not hatred and scorn. The police were holding them back because they wanted to rush forwards and embrace her, not maul her to death.

She didn't understand. But then, all of a sudden, she did. Because beneath the euphoria of her reprieve, something was missing. The crawling, crazing cravings were gone. She no longer thirsted for an ice-cold Mac-Tonic™, and neither did the people. They had gone too long without it; Dwight Eagleman had waited too long. He had overestimated its power, and the people had managed to wriggle free from its slackening grip. They had woken up to its menace.

The revolving door behind Queenie began to move. The reporters were cramming into its compartments. She had to go – but where?

A car horn honked at the roadside, directly ahead. Queenie looked up and caught sight of the driver's face through the glass. She ran between the parted crowds, away from the journalists tumbling out of the courthouse, and the people surged forwards in her wake, breaking through the cordon and meeting in the middle – as though Queenie was a zipper drawing two pieces of colourful fabric together.

She ran around the back of the car and jumped into the passenger seat.

'Where to?' Todd asked.

'Just drive,' Queenie said.

Todd pulled away from the kerb and accelerated along the street. The chaos outside the courthouse receded. He drove, without any destination in mind, until they reached a coastal road.

'They'll come after us, you know?' Todd said.

Queenie nodded. 'I know.'

Todd adjusted his grip on the steering wheel. He checked the rear-view mirror, but couldn't tell whether they were being followed.

'So . . . what next?'

'It'd been nice to go home,' Queenie said, 'but I guess that's what they'll be expecting me to do.'

'I guess.'

Queenie took a deep breath, drank in the sea air.

'You know, nobody will believe that Mac-Tonic™ and Delixir™ are the same thing,' she said. 'That Delixir™ is just as bad.'

A smile spread across Todd's face. 'They will if we can prove it.'

Queenie laughed, but it wasn't such a crazy idea.

'Maybe tomorrow,' she said. 'But not today.'

'Agreed.' Todd said. 'So where to today?'

Queenie looked out at the Pacific Ocean, glinting all the way to the horizon.

'Well, we can't get much farther west.'

Todd nodded. He drove in silence until they merged with the traffic on the interstate, heading east.

*   *   *

Dwight Eagleman was scalping strawberries with an ivory-handled knife when the verdict came in. He paused with the blade against the soft red flesh, frowned at the TV slightly, and then sent the tufty green crown tumbling into the bowl.

Oh well, he thought, picking up another strawberry. *There's always the Mac-Tonic™ time machine.*

EPILOGUE

The Dregs

Bruce Dillinger lifted a finger to his ear and adopted the most serious expression he could muster. After a few seconds of silence, he leaned in and stared down the barrel of the camera.

'We can now go live to Sally, our Pacific correspondent, who has the latest on a breaking story. Over to you, Sally.'

Sally's face appeared beside Bruce's. She beamed like she'd just won the lottery, and it was no wonder: her usual assignments covered hurricanes, tsunamis and volcanic eruptions, but today she appeared to be standing in a tropical paradise. A copse of palm trees swayed gently behind her, and beyond them the sky was an unbroken expanse of brilliant azure.

'Thanks, Bruce. I'm standing on the shore of a tiny island in the middle of the Pacific Ocean – so small, in fact, that it doesn't even have a name. And by all accounts this island should be uninhabited, but if you look just over there . . .'

Sally turned to her right, and the camera swung to follow her gaze. It panned across the beach, revealing a thick blanket of trash that stretched as far as the eye could see. But among the detritus, fifty yards or so from where Sally stood, something crouched: a silhouette against the dazzling horizon.

Bruce squinted at his studio monitor.

'What is that, Sally?'

Sally didn't answer; she was already wading through the trash, her microphone held out before her like the flaming torch of an intrepid explorer. The cameraman followed close behind, stumbling and staggering and struggling to keep the scene in focus. The footage bobbed and blurred, and it was only when Sally came to a stop, and the camera could be steadied, that the dark shape materialized once more.

'Sally?' Bruce said. 'What is that? It looks like a . . .'

The words dried up on Bruce's tongue. Up close, the shape suddenly separated into two distinct figures.

Sally clutched the microphone against her chest. She inhaled deeply, bracing herself against the impossibility of what she was seeing. Then, in a voice

319

that carried across the whole island, she announced her presence.

'Aloha!'

The two figures looked up suddenly, like a couple of startled crows, and the sun hit their faces.

They were both men: that much was clear from their long, frizzy beards. Their lips were dry and cracked, their eyes were wild and their hair hung down past their shoulders. But the strangest thing of all was their attire. They wore no shoes, but both men appeared to be wearing suits – at least, they had been suits once upon a time. The shirts were a sweat-stained yellow, and the jacket sleeves and trouser legs were shredded to rags. They wore silk ties around their heads to keep the hair out of their eyes.

And on the left lapel of each jacket, shiny as the day it was made, was a red bottle-cap badge, with the Mac-Tonic™ logo looping elegantly across the middle.

It was Lyle Funderburk and Lewie Hewitt.

'Mr Funderburk!' Sally said. 'Mr Hewitt! Welcome back to the world of the living! Your actions have caused quite a stir back home – what prompted you to send that message in a bottle?'

Sally's enthusiasm was overpowering at the best of times, but for two lonely castaways deprived of social contact it was like being battered by a sudden typhoon. The two men stared at their sun-scorched feet. Sally was undeterred.

'Can you describe the events that caused your planes to crash?'

One of the bedraggled executives mumbled something unintelligible, but their bushy beards made it impossible to tell who had spoken. Sally didn't miss a beat.

'I think what our viewers would really like to know is how you managed to survive for so long on such a desolate little island?'

Lyle Funderburk and Lewie Hewitt glanced at each other, and then their eyes slid to the carpet of plastic bottles surrounding them.

They didn't say a word, but the secret of their survival was clear enough. It was written in their sheepish expressions, and Sally's slackening smile, and the mounting horror that twisted Bruce Dillinger's face into a grimace.

They'd drunk the dregs, trapped in the washed-up bottles. They'd survived by drinking trickles of warm, sweet Mac-Tonic™ saliva.

Afterword

This book is a work of fiction, which means I made up a lot of things while writing it. The Statue of Liberty, for example, still carries a torch, which remains a symbol of hope and enlightenment around the world; General Sherman has not yet been reduced to a conference table – he continues to grow in Sequoia National Park, California; and 'moonvertising' eludes even the most ambitious corporations – for the time being, at least.

But there are elements of the book that are not a product of my imagination, no matter how much I wish they were. Perhaps the most troubling real-world elements of *Pop!* are the environmental crises it features: the dead zones, the Great Pacific Garbage Patch, global warming. These disasters are happening right now, and yet the priority of big business remains the pursuit of profit – all too often at the expense of the planet.

If you are a child reading this, you are too young to vote (or stand for election), and too young to earn and spend money. As a result, you are less important to politicians and companies than adults, whose votes and money they need to survive. Perhaps this is why they are gambling your future so recklessly: you have the least power to call out their bad bets.

And yet, in many ways, you are the most powerful people in society. Because although you may be too young to participate in politics, you are not too young to be political. You are old enough to ask questions, you are old enough to protest, and you are old enough to make your voice heard. There is something supremely powerful about a child telling a grown-up off, because grown-ups are supposed to know best.

But they don't.

So you mustn't leave it to the adults. The adults are the ones who got us into this mess. And many adults are pinning their hopes on environmental solutions that have not yet been invented, and may never be invented. They are making a problem of today into a bigger problem for tomorrow. In other words, the adults are counting on you to fix their problems.

The trouble is, it may be too late to fix these problems by the time you reach adulthood, which is why you have to act now.

Speak up, and fight back. Educate yourself about the climate and ecological emergency. Take action. Join a movement. Start a new one. Bring your friends. Don't give up after the first defeat. Don't stop after the first victory. Keep going. Demand more. Consume less. Reduce, reuse, recycle. Rebel. Say no until they say yes. Protect your future.

It's your world too.

Mitch Johnson, 2021

Acknowledgements

Thanks to my wife, Harriet, who told me to write when all I wanted was to spend my annual leave feeling sorry for myself; I honestly thought you'd tell me to take two weeks off. Half of *Pop!* was written in that fortnight, and as much as I'd hate to live that fortnight again, I am very glad that I lived it once. Thanks also for looking after a tiny human being while I wrestled imaginary alligators in the shed.

I owe so much to my daughter, Evie, whose aversion to sleep allowed me to inhabit the frazzled, devil-may-care attitude intrinsic to this novel. You give me the best reason to write, and I hope you enjoy *Pop!* when you are old enough to read it. In the meantime, feel free to sleep.

Thanks to Chris and Jol for always being so helpful. You give me time to write and – just as importantly – time to recover. Do you think you could babysit next Wednesday? The laundry's also beginning to pile up . . .

Thanks to my Waterstones colleagues for supporting me and accommodating my literary endeavours. It can't be easy working with someone so demanding and workshy, but thanks for never saying so to my face.

Thanks to my agent, Felicity Trew, who remained remarkably upbeat even when it felt like the worst was happening. You found *Pop!* an excellent home, and I am endlessly grateful for the faith you put in me and my writing.

Huge thanks to Tig Wallace, my editor, who took on a manuscript (and perhaps a writer) that must have seemed like a lot of work. You were undeterred by the book's savagery, and helped me to tame it without extracting any sharp teeth. Your insightful suggestions improved the novel immensely, and your humour and positivity made cutting entire chapters and beloved characters a joy. (Still not over it.)

Thanks to Becca Allen for spotting so many of my mistakes – your meticulous work saved me oodles of embarrassment, and made *Pop!* much more enjoyable to consume.

This book would not exist without the efforts of so many people at Hachette Children's Group, and my deepest thanks go to: Hilary Murray Hill, Kate Agar,

Sarah Lambert, Ruth Alltimes, Nic Goode, Katherine Fox, Jen Hudson, Minnie Tindall, Jemimah James, Imy Clarke, Amina Youssef, Helen Hughes, Hannah Cawse, Flic Highet, Dom Kingston, Tracy Phillips, Annabel El-Kerim, Eshara Wijetunge, Emma Martinez and the rest of the rights team. Lynne Manning designed the perfect cover, and Alice Brereton furnished it with bold and beautiful illustrations. Thank you all for making *Pop!* the shiny, sparkling joyride to Armageddon that it is.

Thanks to Bloomsbury and Seven Stories Press for allowing me to use the Kurt Vonnegut quote at the beginning of this book, and thanks to Kurt Vonnegut for writing those wise words (and countless others) in the first place.

And finally, thanks to X, my spy on the inside.

Also available as
an audio book!

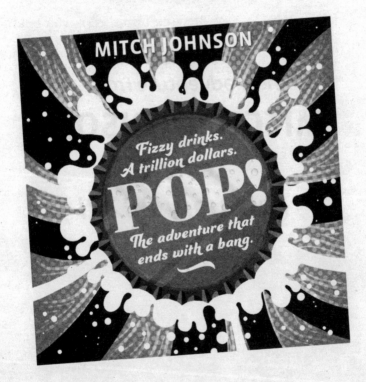

Don't miss the
new adventure from

MITCH JOHNSON,

coming
February 2022!